"I'm not ev... debauch ... mysen property..."

Macy flashed a sexy little grin at Griffin. "So I might need some instruction. But I just think, if we're going to be in Sin City anyway…" She shrugged.

"Go on," he urged, wanting her to spell it out.

"We ought to take advantage."

"I'm going to need specifics," Griffin said, forcing his tone to stay casual.

She crossed her leg toward him and leaned closer. "You, me and a hotel room. No faking it. Is that specific enough?"

Macy's voice had taken on a sensual quality that left no room for doubt. If Griffin had been a guy on the cover of a romance novel, he was pretty sure this was the part where he was supposed to take the woman in his arms, rip the bodice of her dress and start showering her with hungry kisses.

"No faking it," he echoed, his mouth suddenly dry. Yep, that was definitely specific enough…and the best idea he'd heard in years!

ROMANCE

Dear Reader,

While there may not be an actual scientific study proving
that sex makes us dumber, it's hard not to notice that the
phenomenon occurs in a general and immeasurable way
in our lives. But when I got the idea for a study giving
hard evidence about the dumbing-down effects of sex
for our heroine to use to her advantage, I knew I had to
pursue the story.

And what better place for her to throw caution aside and
rob the hero of a few IQ points than Las Vegas? It is, after
all, the place that markets itself as a playground for doing
all the naughty things we otherwise would not do. But
that saying "What happens in Vegas stays in Vegas" never
works out as it's supposed to, does it?

I hope you enjoy *The Sex Quotient*. I'd love to hear
your thoughts on the story. You can reach me at
Jamie@jamiesobrato.com, and you can learn about all
my upcoming Harlequin Blaze novels at my Web site,
www.jamiesobrato.com.

Sincerely,

Jamie Sobrato

THE SEX QUOTIENT
Jamie Sobrato

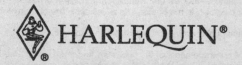

HARLEQUIN®

TORONTO • NEW YORK • LONDON
AMSTERDAM • PARIS • SYDNEY • HAMBURG
STOCKHOLM • ATHENS • TOKYO • MILAN • MADRID
PRAGUE • WARSAW • BUDAPEST • AUCKLAND

ISBN-13: 978-0-373-79270-2
ISBN-10:   0-373-79270-0

THE SEX QUOTIENT

ABOUT THE AUTHOR

Jamie Sobrato lives in Southern California and writes for Harlequin Blaze. *The Sex Quotient* is her tenth novel. She has never debauched herself in Las Vegas, in spite of numerous trips to that mecca of sinfulness, and she swears she would not ever try to dumb down a guy with sex. Well, at least not on purpose.

Books by Jamie Sobrato

HARLEQUIN TEMPTATION

HARLEQUIN BLAZE

To Janet Erazo-Sloat,
for being a lifelong friend from the start

1

"MY STUDY proves it—sex makes us dumb."

Macy Thomaston leaned in close to make sure her friend could hear her over the noise in the downtown San Francisco bar. "You needed to spend the past three years of your life researching to figure that out?"

Lauren Parish shook her head. "Not dumb like you're thinking. What I mean is, we literally lose IQ points every time we have an orgasm."

Macy stared at her friend, a sense of outrage rising in her chest. "When you became a medical researcher, I thought you were going to discover cures for serious illnesses, not ruin my sex life."

Lauren, who, up until a few seconds ago, had been one of Macy's favorite people in the world, dismissed her concern with a shrug. "Knowledge is power."

Macy glanced around the Irish pub at the disappointing selection of single men. "Maybe that's what's wrong with all the men I've dated lately. Too much sex."

"Seriously," Lauren said. "It's all about biochemistry." She pushed some papers across the table. "Read the concluding paragraph."

Macy flipped through the pages of the study Lauren had just finished drafting until she came to the end. And there it was, laid out in medical jargon, soon to be published in the *Journal of American Medicine*—that biochemicals released during orgasm have a temporary dumbing-down effect on the human brain. Weakened recall skills, sluggish thought processes, even a brief drop in IQ had been noted among the research subjects.

"I can't believe you've proven this," Macy said as a waitress brushed past, dropping a green flyer of the bar's weekly events on the table.

"So what do you think?"

"I think you're going to piss off the world," Macy said, her mind whirring with the possibilities.

"Of course, but what do you *really* think? Does it freak you out a little? Make you want to change your behavior at all?"

"I don't know. I'm just stunned."

Lauren sipped her beer. "I, for one, will be a lot more careful about the timing of my sexual encounters. I mean, think about it—"

"You've got a big job interview or an important meeting Monday morning, so that means no hot sex Saturday night," Macy said, her bewilderment growing.

Would this mean the end of casual sex as she knew it?

"Exactly. And since the effects last up to four days, any important mental challenge in the early part of the work week could ruin entire weekends of potential sex."

"Unless it's bad sex, right?"

Lauren laughed. "That seems to be the case. The

stronger the orgasm, the more noticeable the effects. And study subjects who had no orgasm at all experienced no negative reactions."

Around them, blue-collar regulars at the bar mixed with the growing crowd of yuppies who'd recently discovered O'Shaunnessy's and declared it authentic and therefore a cool place to be seen. *Authentic* was certainly one way to describe the grungy hardwood floors, the slightly sticky tables and the malt scent that filled the air. The bartenders had Irish accents, and the waitresses wore skin-tight jeans.

Macy, still in her pale yellow wool summer suit, and Lauren, in her standard black pants and black top, with her long brown hair gleaming in the dim light, were guilty of being from the searching-for-authenticity side of the crowd.

"Oh God," Macy said, the reality of the findings settling in her brain. "We can have sex before the big meeting, but we can't come."

"Not if you want to be at your best, you shouldn't."

"This is so depressing. Why'd you even have to do this stupid study, anyway?" Macy asked.

"Because it will make my career?"

"You should find a new career—something outside of medical research—before you discover that chocolate is the singular cause of cellulite or something equally horrifying."

"Try to look on the bright side. Now that you know the truth about sex, you can use it to your advantage."

"Right, so when I need to become dumb and forgetful, I just have to go get laid. That's *so* helpful to know."

"No, when you need your *boyfriend* to become dumb and forgetful, you just need to screw his brains out."

"I'll be sure to use the information for my own evil purposes next chance I get."

"Seriously, you should! The results of the study won't hit mainstream media for at least another few months."

Macy sighed. "Too bad I don't have a boyfriend," she said without really meaning it. Being a career girl of the overachieving variety meant she'd been too busy for a boyfriend lately, and she didn't need a guy hanging around just to tell her she worked too hard, anyway.

"There are probably a hundred men here tonight who'd be happy to remedy that problem."

Macy was occasionally caught off guard by the fact that men found her attractive. Even after ten years of being thin, blond and decidedly coquettish, within her lurked the kid who'd had to wear the chubby sizes from the Sears kids' department.

"I just need the sex, not the guy. But now you've ruined even that for me. Could you remind me why we're friends again?"

"Because I always embarrass myself when I get drunk, and you like to watch the spectacle."

That much was true. And at the rate Lauren was going tonight, she'd be creating a spectacle in another twenty minutes or so.

"How good are you at faking it?"

Macy looked at Lauren, for a moment confused about whether she meant faking orgasms or faking any sort of enthusiasm for the bar scene tonight. "It's not something I do often, but I can call upon my acting skills if I have to," she said.

Around them, the crowd was getting rowdier by the drink. Wednesday was Ladies' Night, and people were celebrating the middle of the week as if they meant it.

"We're at O'Shaunnessy's—AKA the Big O—and that means there's a fake-orgasm contest starting in a half hour," Lauren said in a tone that would have been more appropriate for offering Macy a fudge brownie sundae, and now she knew to what sort of faking her friend referred.

"I'm supposed to be tempted by that because?"

"Because you should enter. Given the results of my study, I'd say we're all going to have to hone our acting skills sooner or later."

"Um...no."

"C'mon, it'll be fun. I'll enter too—it's the perfect way to celebrate my having finished the study."

"Now *that* I'd like to see. I could definitely get cheered up by you faking it in front of all these guys."

"I bet my fake orgasm's way better than your fake orgasm."

Macy resisted a smile. She had to hand it to Lauren—she knew how to cheer a girl up. And after a miserable day like today, Macy seriously needed cheering.

She eyed the dance floor, where one of the bar employees was setting up a small platform and a microphone. "I'm pretty sure I haven't had enough to drink to fake an orgasm into a microphone in front of several hundred people."

Lauren shooed away her protest. "You'll be great."

Macy hadn't been great today when she'd needed to be. Then again, it wasn't her style to feel sorry for herself, or to let a guy like Griffin Reed get the best of her. She'd think of a way to get him back for making her look like an idiot in front of everyone at Bronson and Wade. But first, she needed to unwind, to stop thinking about the world of advertising for a while.

"I'm going to sign us up. I'll be right back."

"No!" Macy said, to no avail.

As her friend disappeared, she found herself sitting alone with her drink at the bar, suddenly an easy target for the barflies. And she was far from in the mood to field pick-up lines.

Her inner chubby girl wanted to go home and curl up on the couch with a pepperoni pizza. Macy might be thin now—in the best shape of her life actually, thanks to living far away from her food-equals-love mother and sticking with a torturous workout regimen—and she might be blond, thanks to the skill of her beloved hair stylist, but surface changes could only go so far past skin-deep.

The ingenue act she'd mastered to go with her polished look was just that—an act designed to distract the world from the fact that Macy wasn't nearly as sure of herself as everyone expected her to be.

Working in advertising, she knew the importance of packaging, the irresistible lure of a glossy, attractive appearance. And she knew how to project that shiny happy appearance to the world, even when she was feeling anything but. However, when Griffin Reed was involved, sometimes she faltered.

Today had been a case in point. Instead of standing up to Griffin when he'd made her look as though she possessed the creativity of a cucumber during a brain-storming session with their entire creative team, she'd simply let him have all the glory. And if that's how little spine she possessed, she deserved the humiliation she got.

She and Griffin were competing for the same promotion to creative director, and she wanted it at least as badly as he did. Yet she let her faltering confidence sabotage her when it counted most. Lack of confidence kept her from taking risks, and in the world of advertising, willingness to take risks meant the difference between success and failure.

She had to buckle up and show everyone that she had what it took to lead the creative team. What she might sometimes lack in confidence, she made up for in her ability to think outside the box. She could, and would, take the risks needed.

She'd been the leader of the art department for two years now, and while she liked her job, she didn't feel challenged enough. She wanted to feel as though she was living up to her full potential. She wanted to shape the entire vision on their projects, not just one aspect of it. She knew she had what it took—her ideas were often the most visionary in the office—but everyone considered Griffin a shoo-in for the promotion.

He was the head of the copywriting department, and he'd been at Bronson and Wade three years longer than Macy. He had enough confidence for ten people, and that made him look more capable than he actually was. Sure, he did his job well, but he wasn't nearly as talented as Macy.

But everyone loved Griffin. He was an all-star American-jock kind of guy, and everywhere he went people flocked around him, just as in high school, where guys like him had gotten all the attention and ignored girls like her.

She stared into the crowd until Lauren emerged from it. When she caught Macy's expression, her friend offered a weak smile.

"You've got twenty minutes to liquor up before the orgasm fest begins," Lauren said as she sat down.

"You've mistaken me for a girl who likes to be in the spotlight."

"Don't kid yourself, you love attention. How you act when you're drunk tells the truth."

Macy grimaced, then polished off her vodka tonic. "I'm having an overweight moment."

Lauren made a show of looking around her barstool. "I'm sorry, I don't see a couch here."

"A what?"

"You must have mistaken me for your shrink, but sorry, babe, you need to get over the trauma of not fitting into your prom dress a decade ago."

Macy bit her lip to keep from laughing. No doubt, Lauren knew how to keep it real. "Point taken."

"I don't care how many cookies your mother fed you, you look fabulous now, and you need to act the part of the babe you are."

"I thought you were a proponent of faking it in bed—not in life."

"Here's your chance to fake it in front of an audience. If you tried, you could bring all the men in this bar to their knees."

Macy rolled her eyes. Lauren was exaggerating…or was she? Maybe this stupid orgasm contest was her chance to make up for the lack of confidence she'd displayed at work. Maybe the risk of humiliation would be made up for by the reward of testing her limits. Okay, that was stretching it, but she did need to do something to banish all the negative energy she'd gotten wrapped up in.

"Fine," she said, feeling the stress of the workday finally draining away. "Bring on the microphone."

AFTER WORKING a twelve-hour day, Griffin Reed hadn't been thrilled by the idea of walking an extra four blocks to the out-of-the-way Irish pub his coworker and closest friend at the office, Carson McCullen, claimed was the new hot place to be on Wednesday nights.

All he'd really wanted to do was go home, grab a beer and chill out on the couch. Not exactly the stuff an exciting night was made of, but he was damn tired. Working his ass off to impress the higher-ups at the agency enough to convince them he deserved a promotion left him occasionally wondering if it was all worth it—if getting the promotion would really be the end-all, be-all he'd told himself it would be.

Immediately, the noise and merriment in the bar sapped away a little more of his energy, and he glanced back at the door, wondering how long he'd have to stay before he could politely skip out for the night. Probably he was stuck until Carson found a girl to hook up with.

But the moment Griffin saw Macy Thomaston across the room, he could have danced a freaking jig.

He spotted her at a table near the back with a friend, her long legs peeking out of her skirt, crossed and propped on the bottom rung of her chair. Did she have any idea how distracting her legs were? Did she suspect how often he'd nearly lost his train of thought after catching a glimpse of them in a meeting?

She must have, or she wouldn't have so often made a point of wearing skirts that were cut above the knee.

Did she have the slightest notion how often he'd fantasized about taking her into his office, closing the door, sprawling her on his desk, and pushing her designer skirt up around her waist? Trailing his tongue up her satiny inner thigh—

Damn it, he had to stop.

She'd been the object of his desire for too long, and something had to give. He'd turned her ass and her legs and her tits into his own personal fetishes.

He insisted to Carson they sit in an inconspicuous spot, where he could keep tabs on Macy unnoticed. Seeing her outside of work was a rare treat, and seeing how she behaved around a bunch of horny men when she didn't know she was being watched would be interesting, to say the least.

Not that he was some kind of stalker—he'd let his presence be known after he'd had the chance to observe for a short while. He just wondered what she was like when she wasn't making his life hell at work.

Macy had no idea how hot she was. Or, more likely she did know, and she was extremely good at using what she had to get what she wanted.

"When are you two finally going to screw and get it over with?" Carson asked, his gaze traveling from Macy to Griffin.

Griffin shrugged. "I keep reminding myself that all the fun is in the chase," he said in a tone that didn't sound convincing even to his own ears.

"All the fun is in the panties, man."

"Yeah, but I've gotta *work* with the panties and the girl who lives in them."

"And she might be our supervisor as of next week. Guess that could create problems."

That was one problem Griffin didn't plan to worry about, because *he* was going to get the promotion, not Macy. He ached for the challenge of more responsibility almost as much as he ached for Macy herself.

"Macy's friend is kind of hot. I hope we're not going to hide out over here all damn night, because I'd like to make a move."

"Just give me fifteen minutes." Fifteen minutes to watch, and possibly find some clue about Macy. What, he didn't know. Maybe he'd be able to figure out which part of Macy's vixen persona was an act and which part was for real. But that was probably hoping for too much.

A waitress arrived to take their drink order, then disappeared into the crowd that was growing denser by the minute. All attention seemed to be directed toward a guy with a microphone who hadn't said anything yet.

"I forgot to tell you the best part of this place— every Wednesday, they hold a fake orgasm contest."

"Sounds classy."

The guy at the microphone started talking, introducing the contest, which he claimed was a beloved O'Shaunnessy's tradition. Griffin tuned him out and turned his attention back to Macy's table, but she was no longer there. He glanced around, trying to spot her golden-blond hair in the crowd, but no luck. Her suit jacket was still hanging from the back of her chair, so he knew she hadn't left.

But then he heard the words, "Our first contestant, Macy," and his heart stopped beating in his chest for a few seconds.

There couldn't be two women named Macy in the bar tonight. And then he saw her, standing first in the lineup of women waiting to compete in the orgasm contest.

God help him.

Griffin had never mastered predicting anything about Macy, and his reaction to seeing her ready to take the microphone was just one more example of the many ways she could throw him off guard.

He loved that about her. He loved that just when he thought she was going to weave left, she darted right. Just when he thought she'd turn cold and bitchy, she became flirty and inviting. And he hated that he loved that about her.

Okay, so she was a coworker, and he should never have been flirting with her, should never have set his sights on getting her into bed. But from the first time he'd ever laid eyes on the hot little blonde with the sultry brown eyes and the lush, taste-me lips, he'd wanted her in the undeniable way that made guys do stupid things.

"Could we actually be this lucky," Carson said, "that we get to witness our very own Macy Thomaston pretending to have the big O?"

"It seems too good to be true, doesn't it?" Griffin said, his gaze still locked on her. He couldn't have looked away if someone had set his table on fire.

She stepped up to the microphone, and a song with a sexy dance beat began to play over the speakers. She didn't look drunk or overly afraid. A little half smile played on her lips, and she closed her eyes.

"*Mmmmmmmm*," she purred into the mike, a sound that resonated right between Griffin's legs.

He shifted in his seat, his breath caught in his throat. Her hips were rocking to the beat of the music, creating a show almost as entertaining as her voice was.

"*Oooohhhhhh.*" Her head tilted back, her eyes still closed, one hand gripped the mike and the other traveled up the side of her neck, behind it, and into her long, wavy hair. "*Yesssss... Mmm...*"

She breathed quick and shallow, gasping and crying out, making hot, girly sounds that Griffin had thought up until that moment were too spontaneous, too visceral, for a woman to fake. Her face, transformed by some imagined pleasure, wore the sort of blissed-out expression he'd thought more times than he cared to count that only he could put on a woman.

And then her performance reached its groin-stirring crescendo, with a series of moans and mmm's and yeses that had every guy in the place cheering and whistling. When she finally fell silent, he realized beads of sweat had formed on his temples, and his shirt had grown damp around the collar.

"Damn," Carson said.

"Yeah. Damn."

Part of him wanted to sidle up to Macy's table as soon as she sat down and watch her horrified expression when she realized two of her coworkers had just witnessed her Oscar-worthy performance.

But it wasn't the right move. He knew information like this needed to be saved and used at just the right moment. He wasn't sure what that moment was yet, but he'd find it soon enough.

"Look, man," he said to Carson, "We can't let her see us here."

"Why not?"

"We just can't." Not exactly his most persuasive argument, but he was still in a sexual daze from the show.

"I'm not leaving when the orgasms are just getting started."

A second woman had taken the mike, though she didn't have half of Macy's acting skills.

Griffin stood up and placed enough money on the table to cover his drink and tip. "I'm out of here. Don't let her see you, okay?"

Carson's expression turned annoyed. "How am I going to hook up with her friend without Macy seeing me?"

"Pick another woman, and I'll owe you big-time."

"Fine, go ahead, run off like the wuss you know you are."

Griffin gave Carson a look and headed for the door. His every guy part wanted to go in the other direction though, toward Macy and all the trouble she had to offer. But his guy parts would have to wait.

He'd have Macy, the object of his desire, but only when the time was right.

2

TURNS OUT, Macy was damn good at faking it. Good as in she was beginning to wonder if she'd missed her calling in life. Well, maybe not *that* good, but she'd impressed the crowd at O'Shaunnessy's Pub last night enough to win the weekly fake orgasm contest. It wasn't exactly her proudest accomplishment, but it *had* been a lot more fun than she'd expected.

She placed the silly gold plastic shamrock trophy that had been the prize on her desk, not sure what she'd tell anyone who asked about it or why she'd even brought the thing to work. No, that wasn't true. She knew why she'd brought it to put on her desk—because it was a reminder to be confident, to take risks, to use the talent she had to get where she wanted to go. It was a reminder that she was no longer the chubby nerd, who still haunted her psyche, but was now a girl who could incite a whole bar to whistle and applaud by moaning into a microphone.

She turned her attention to the onslaught of e-mail messages that had somehow invaded her inbox overnight. Bronson and Wade wasn't a huge advertising firm, but the thirty or so people who worked there managed to produce enough interoffice e-mail for a few hundred. She skimmed for important subject lines, and her gaze immediately fell on one entitled, Las Vegas Trip from Griffin Reed.

Just as she opened it, the sender himself appeared at her desk, his sudden presence both pleasant and irritating in that paradoxical way he had. "Are you up for the trip?" he asked.

Macy tried not to be impressed that he could look so gorgeous before noon, but she failed. Griffin, who was maybe a year or two older than her twenty-nine, always looked annoyingly, distractingly good, with his short, dark brown hair and his smoldering gray eyes, his custom-tailored shirts and his Armani suits. He was clearly aware of the fact.

"Why do you even bother with e-mail if you're going to come here and ask me the question anyway?"

"I sent you that two hours ago. I didn't realize you'd be coming to work late today."

She glanced at her watch and confirmed that it was only 9:05 a.m. "I'm not late."

Which he knew, but he loved to bait her. "Right," he said with a little smile. "I forgot you operate on Macy time."

"What do you want? I haven't even had a chance to read your e-mail."

"We got the Golden Gate Resort and Casino account. Now they want a couple of us from the creative team to fly there this weekend and check the place out before we start working on the campaign."

"A couple of us as in whom?" A little sinking feeling descended into Macy's stomach.

"You, me and Carson."

"I'm supposed to spend a weekend in Las Vegas with you and Carson?"

"It's a sweet deal. Free hotel rooms, free meals, VIP service. All we have to do is show up and debauch ourselves."

"I'll leave the debauching to you," she said, but an image from another Vegas hotel's recent ad campaign popped into her head.

A woman, dressed in black lingerie, crawling across a bed to her lover. He stood beside the bed, arms crossed, leaning against a piece of furniture, his expression vaguely pleased, looking as if he could be her client or her lover. The caption read, Embrace the fantasy.

She'd been studying Las Vegas ads ever since she'd first heard the possibility that they could get the Golden Gate Casino account, and that ad had been her favorite. Now she realized why—it appealed to her on a personal level. She was long overdue for a weekend of serious debauchery herself.

Griffin's gaze settled on her shamrock trophy, and he smiled as if he recognized it. "What's that?"

"Oh, nothing," Macy said a little too quickly. "Just a good-luck charm." Which wasn't entirely untrue. The trophy's lucky properties hadn't been established yet, but Macy had a good feeling about the little hunk of plastic.

Besides, she believed in creating her own luck, so if she said the thing was lucky, it was.

Griffin looked as if he were about to say something else about the shamrock, but instead he said, "We'll fly out tomorrow around noon, if you want to go."

"Hmm, tough choice—leave work early and jet off on a free trip to Vegas for the weekend, or stick around here and get indigestion from the Friday-afternoon pizza meeting."

"I thought you'd feel that way." He dropped an airline ticket envelope on her desk.

And then he launched into a discourse on his ideas for the campaign. Blah blah blah. Griffin had a way of sounding sure of himself, sure his ideas were perfect, while at the same time never listening to anyone else.

Still, Macy found him ridiculously attractive. That, she just didn't understand.

Never had, never would.

Ever since they'd first met there had been tension. Not always the hostile kind—more often than not, the sexual kind—but always enough to make working together difficult. And rather than being annoyed by their relationship, Griffin seemed to relish it.

Macy realized a moment too late that Griffin was staring at her for an answer about she-didn't-know-what.

"What's with the spaced-out look?" he said.

"You just caught me at a bad time. It's a little early for me to be thinking creatively."

"You weren't even paying attention." He smiled, and his eyes crinkled at the corners.

He always smelled great, and now, with his close proximity as he leaned against her desk, Macy could smell his spicy guy scent all too well. If she'd had to come up with a marketing spin for it, she'd have called it the scent of an alpha male.

She hated that she found him so damn attractive, hated that she loved the way his wavy brown hair always looked perfectly tousled, hated that his mouth was so sensual, so worthy of staring at for hours on end.

And she especially hated that she often caught herself wondering how he'd feel molded against her, acting out all the stupid fantasies she'd had about him when she hadn't had anyone better to fantasize about— and a few times when she had.

"You weren't saying anything I needed to pay attention to."

"If we're going to work together on this account, you should at least pretend to respect my ideas."

"You're right," she said with a little smile. "I'll be sure to pretend extra hard."

"I think you're just feeling disgruntled that you've got stiff competition for the creative director job."

Macy shrugged. "A little healthy competition can be a good thing, right?"

"Right. Just remember that when I get the account."

That was Griffin's fatal flaw—overconfidence. And that was how she'd bring him down.

She turned to her computer and cast him a glance. "I really need to get some work done here."

"Fine," he said. "See you at the ten o'clock meeting."

And then he was gone as fast as he'd shown up. No sticking around to ask her off-the-wall questions, no flirting, nothing.

Something was up, but it was too early in the morning for Macy to figure out what right now. Give her a few more cups of coffee and a few more hours, and she'd figure out what was going on. If nothing else, she'd grill Griffin later. For now she had all these e-mail messages to plow through. And work to wrap up before tomorrow.

When she'd be flying to Vegas.

The thought gave her a ridiculous little thrill. She was going to Las Vegas with Griffin, going to the one place where it was okay to be bad, where, if you got yourself into trouble, you could blame it on the city, on the booze, on the bright neon lights.

Not that Macy had any intention of getting into trouble, but somehow, she realized as she stared at her little shamrock trophy perched on her desk, it seemed inevitable that something was going to happen.

Something risky. Something wild. Something that could only happen in Las Vegas.

Lauren's awful study popped into her head out of the blue. Then came the comment Lauren had made about Macy using the information for her own benefit before it became general knowledge.

When Macy had said she'd use the study results for her own evil purposes the next chance she got, she'd been kidding. She'd never imagined she might really have some nefarious plan to plot out.

A plan like the one forming in the sleep-fogged recesses of her brain right now. It was probably too crazy to give another second's thought to.

Or was it?

What if…

What if she gave in to the lure of Las Vegas? What

if she gave in to the attraction she'd been fighting for the past year, in the name of career advancement?

What if she could seduce Griffin out of a few IQ points? If she had the chance, would she even have the nerve to try? Last night, she'd proven to herself that she had the nerve to try just about anything.

If Griffin could stoop to using sex as his weapon—always flirting with her to distract her—then she could do it for one weekend. Only her weapon was sharper than his, and she was aiming it right where it would hurt the most—at his intellect.

Could it really be so easy?

Maybe it could. She turned her attention back to her computer, but before she could even open another message, someone cleared their throat beside her desk. She looked up to see Griffin there again.

"I forgot to ask, are you going to come in to work tomorrow?"

"I'll probably just work from home in the morning."

"Do you want a car to pick you up for the airport? If so, I'll just need your address to give to the limo service."

"Hmm, a limo," she said. "That could be fun." She purposely let her gaze travel over him as a little smile played on her lips. "Will you be in it?"

Shock registered in his eyes, but he quickly recovered. "Yeah, but so will Carson."

"Too bad."

His usual annoying smirk was gone, replaced by an inscrutable expression. If forced to name it, Macy would have to say it was desire.

He looked as if he was seriously hot and bothered. Perfect!

She resisted the urge to rub her hands together in mock diabolical style. Macy had the distinct feeling of having just offered a sugary-sweet treat to a hungry toddler. A little bubble of guilt threatened to rise up in her chest and spoil her fun, but she ignored it.

How many times had Griffin upstaged her, purposely made her look like an idiot in front of management and used his own sex appeal to manipulate every female within a ten-office radius of him? More than Macy could count.

If she wanted to get ahead competing with Griffin, she'd have to get over the guilt. Guys like him didn't feel guilty about things like this, and she had to think like him. Beat him at his own game.

"Why isn't the intern doing this grunt work? Are you looking for reasons to drop by my desk?"

"The intern's out sick today, and this trip just came up last second," he said, ignoring her taunt.

She found some paper and a pen on her desk, then wrote out driving directions to her house.

Griffin leaned on the table and watched as she wrote. "Marina District?" he asked.

Macy nodded handed the paper to him. "I lucked into a rent-controlled loft. If I lean out my living-room window, I can almost see the Golden Gate Bridge."

He smiled. "A place with a view—what more can you ask for in the city?"

"Indoor plumbing is always a plus."

"Oh yeah, that too."

"And neighbors that don't belong to any cults or secret societies."

"Well, now you're just getting picky."

Macy laughed. "You've adapted well to the city. It's a far cry from your hometown."

Macy knew from talk around the office that Griffin had moved from Wilmington, North Carolina, to San Francisco right after college when he'd taken the job at Bronson and Wade three years before she'd been hired. Macy had wished more than a few times that he'd pack up and go back to the tobacco farm where he belonged. Even the ever-so-slight Southern lilt that remained in his voice only served to make him more infuriatingly sexy.

"North Carolina isn't so different from here," he said. "There's an ocean there, and lots of bad drivers."

"Do you ever miss it?"

"Nah. There's a reason so many people crowd into this one tiny part of the country."

"Because it's the best damn city in the world."

"Right, and full of such modest locals." He grinned.

"So you're going to make this your permanent home?"

He nodded. "When I get that promotion next week, I'll be able to afford a house."

When. Not if. Arrogant bastard. He assumed no one could beat him, no one was more talented than him and no one deserved the promotion more than he did.

Whatever misguided feelings of guilt might have been lingering vanished, and Macy knew without a doubt that she was doing the right thing. She'd sex

Griffin out of a few IQ points, and he'd never know what hit him. It would give her the edge she needed to distract attention from Griffin's oh-so-distracting presence, and then…

Then she'd have a fighting chance.

If she had her way, by the end of the weekend, Griffin Reed would be so dumbed down by sex, all of his best ad ideas would involve dancing bears and monkeys in tuxedoes.

MACY GLANCED at her watch. It was five minutes after twelve, and the creative team sat around the meeting room table, waiting for the endless ten o'clock meeting to finally wrap up. She hated these state-of-the-business meetings, where the partners took every opportunity to make the creative team feel as if they knew nothing about business and had no talent. It was their covert strategy, everyone believed, for keeping them from overestimating their value, asking for raises, or daring to look elsewhere for employment.

She had lost the ability to focus on what anyone was saying about thirty minutes ago, when her stomach had started rumbling and her desire for a cheeseburger had overpowered every other thought.

Across the table, Griffin appeared to be riveted to Gordon Bronson's summary of the agency's current accounts, and Macy was trying really hard not to look at him and imagine what sort of Las Vegas debauchery she might be involved in with him very soon. That seemed to be the only thought that distracted her from craving a cheeseburger.

She was afraid whatever she imagined about Griffin would be revealed on her face, and the last thing she needed was him getting all overconfident about her sexual attraction to him before they'd even gotten away from the office. She knew him—he'd find a way to use it against her.

"And our final item to address," Gordon was saying, "is the matter of the vacant position of creative director."

Macy snapped to attention, her brain suddenly disinterested in Griffin and lunch.

"And I see we have our two prime candidates sitting right across from each other, facing off just as they should be," Gordon said, then laughed.

Around the table, forced chuckles could be heard, and Macy herself smiled at Griffin in a way she imagined made her look as though she was sitting on tacks. He gazed back at her, vaguely amused, probably already patting himself on the back mentally for having the job in the bag.

"I'm hoping in the next week we'll see something brilliant out of one of you to make the decision a little easier."

"Absolutely, sir," Griffin said.

Macy nodded, as if she didn't mind at all being treated like a racehorse rather than a human being. Truth be told, she thought Gordon Bronson was an utter and complete asshole, but it wasn't like that opinion was going to get her a promotion or a raise, so she knew how to stay quiet about it.

"I'll expect to see an impressive start on the Golden Gate account—from both of you. Don't forget for a second that you're competing for the same job, and may the best ad man or woman win," Gordon said.

Macy tried not to roll her eyes, and when she got past the urge, she caught Griffin surreptitiously doing the very thing she'd been avoiding.

Griffin thought Gordon Bronson was an ass, too? Could it really be? She'd never dared to broach the subject in real life, but it comforted her in some small way to know she wasn't the only one.

She suppressed a laugh, bit the inside of her cheek and thought about how much she would owe this year on her taxes to get rid of any humorous impulses. The urge to laugh passed, and she tried to focus again on what the senior partner had to say.

But just then, Griffin caught her eye, and he pinned her with one of his looks that was nearly dripping with sex. Her traitorous body responded with a little wave of heat. He had such an uncanny way of tripping her up with those looks at the most inopportune times, as if he knew he could use his sex appeal to distract her when she least expected it.

Damn him.

"And Macy, by the way…"

Macy sat up straighter, her heart flip-flopping at being addressed in front of everyone at the table. She looked at Gordon. "Yes, sir?"

"I thought your team's recent work on the Blaudren campaign was a bit disappointing. If you really want to be competitive for the promotion, you're going to have to thoroughly impress us in the next week. Show us you can be more of a risk-taker, more of an innovator than some of your more predictable work has suggested."

She felt her face burning, and she slumped a bit. "Okay, Mr. Bronson. I'm sure I can deliver," she said, not sure how convincing she sounded.

She'd considered her work on the Blaudren campaign some of her best, but that was the thing about Gordon—he had rather unpredictable tastes, and sometimes he liked to insult people's work just for the fun of it, it seemed. Or maybe to push them to try harder.

She heard nothing for the final five minutes of the meeting, as her brain raced around the idea that she was lower on the promotion totem pole than Griffin now.

If she didn't get the promotion, Macy was going to be seriously disillusioned with her own abilities. She'd proven time and again that she was worthy of more responsibility, and she'd proven to herself that she could take the risks necessary to move up in her career, even if Gordon didn't think so. If she didn't get the job, she feared she'd be right back at square one, her confidence crushed, her self-esteem lowered to chubby high-school nerd levels again.

She could not go that low again.

While she was wrapped up in her own thoughts, Gordon finally closed the meeting, and the senior partners bustled out of the boardroom. The creative team was still sitting around, discussing details that had come up, and making lunch plans, while Macy sat in a stupor, feeling like a bit of an ass for being the only one who'd been called out for less than stellar work.

A paper airplane sailed across the table and landed

next to Macy's notebook. She looked up in the direction it had come from—Griffin's direction, of course—and found him staring at her smugly.

"Don't be mad," he said. "I'm sure you can recover from that Blaudren debacle."

"Thanks for the vote of confidence," she said sarcastically.

From somewhere to the right, someone snickered. Probably Lynn Baxter, Macy's arch nemesis, who relished watching Griffin upstage her. She refused to give Lynn the satisfaction of even a glance in her direction.

Instead, Macy picked up the paper airplane, aimed it at Griffin's head when he glanced away at Lynn, and sent it sailing through the air with a flick of her wrist. The plane zoomed toward its target at a surprising speed, and as if Macy had orchestrated the whole scene, just as Griffin turned toward her again, the tip of the plane crashed into his forehead, bounced off and landed on the boardroom table.

Everyone in the room laughed, and she could see a little rush of color in Griffin's cheeks. He pinned her with his sex-loaded gaze again, and the heat there nearly melted her in her chair. God, she hated how he could do that in a split second, even when she was pissed off at him. Even when she'd just pelted him with a paper airplane.

How the hell did he do that?

"Am I sensing a little hostility?" he asked, the corner of his mouth curving up.

Thank goodness that's *all* he sensed coming from her right now with their coworkers watching.

She forced an even smile. "I have no idea what you're talking about. That airplane just slipped right out of my hand."

"Yeah," Carson said, recovering from his laughter. "I saw it. It slipped."

Griffin rubbed the spot where the plane had hit him.

"Just remember," he said. "I'll be a fair boss. I won't hold petty things like this against you after I get the promotion—I promise."

His self-satisfied smile spoke volumes about his conviction that he would, indeed, be the next creative director. He didn't have a doubt in the world.

Macy's first instinct was to lash out with a smart-ass comment of her own, but she held back. She had to keep the big picture in mind. No matter how much he might piss her off today, tomorrow she'd get hers.

Tomorrow, and all weekend, she'd see to it that Griffin finally got what was coming to him. He'd never know what hit him, and it definitely wouldn't be a paper airplane.

3

TRYING TO JAM a full day's work into two hours this morning before he'd gone back home, fed his cat enough to last a weekend, put out an extra litter box and caught a limo to pick up Macy and Carson, had left Griffin feeling a little harried.

Not to mention the pressure that was mounting over the impending promotion announcement at work. He could almost feel the partners sizing him up at any given moment, could sense their satisfaction with his performance, but there was still the what-if factor going on. What if they didn't choose him? Could he even stay at Bronson and Wade in that case? Could he keep on working in a job where he didn't feel challenged enough, where he wanted more autonomy but couldn't have it? He didn't want to face any of those possibilities now, not when he was so close to having the promotion in the bag. He wasn't twenty-five anymore, and he still had a lot to prove, including the fact that he could handle more responsibility.

And now that he was finally alone with Macy, he felt a second wind coming on.

Griffin shoved his carry-on bag into the overhead bin,

then sat in the seat next to Macy's. Carson had volunteered to get bumped from their flight because of overbooking and catch another a half hour later, which was fine with Griffin. A few hours alone together in first class would give him a chance to have a little fun with Macy.

She had her nose buried in a book, pretending to be engrossed in it, but he knew better. She was just trying to avoid talking to him. She wore a white suit and pink lace camisole, and Griffin couldn't help admiring her finer attributes for a moment as he leaned in close and pretended to be interested in what she was reading.

She smelled a little like cotton candy, his favorite carnival treat, and he wondered if it was the perfume she wore, or some kind of flavored body lotion. Did she taste as sweet as she smelled?

He'd debated all day about when and if to reveal he'd seen her little orgasm act. And, impatient guy that he was, he didn't see the point of waiting any longer.

"*Mmmmm,*" he said, low enough so only she could hear.

She looked up and frowned. "Are you eating something?"

No, but he'd like to be. "I was just admiring how well you fake it."

Her expression turned from perplexed to wary. "What are you talking about?"

"You weren't really reading that book, were you?"

"Of course I was."

"You just didn't want to have to talk to me."

She snapped the book closed. The title of it was

Wicked Pleasures, one of those novels with a frilly-looking cover featuring a guy and a girl in the throes of passion.

"What would you like to talk about?"

He smiled. "Good book?"

She shrugged. "It's okay."

"Did you get to the part where they do that?" he asked, nodding to the passionate half-clothed embrace.

"Yeah, but honestly, they do a lot more than *that.*"

"Does the girl ever fake it?"

Some of the color drained from her face. "Fake *what?* Why do you keep talking about faking it?"

He plucked the in-flight magazine from the back of the seat in front of him and pretended to be interested in it. "No reason."

"Griffin, what the hell are you talking about?"

"Do you have an air purifier in your apartment?" He asked as he pretended to study an ad for one.

He glanced up and caught her looking as though she might bolt from the airplane.

"Did you go to O'Shaunnessy's Wednesday night?" she asked

Smart girl—he had to give her that.

"Why do you ask?" he said, trying hard not to smile.

She seemed to give the matter some thought. And then some small *something* about her changed. Her posture, her color, her expression... He couldn't put his finger on what it was, but she didn't look freaked out anymore.

"You were there," she said.

"There for what?"

"For my orgasm."

The guy in the seat in front of them glanced back with interest.

And there it was again—Macy's complete unpredictability. Just when he thought he was going to embarrass the hell out of her, she got all calm and matter-of-fact.

"It was an impressive performance," he said.

She smiled. "Glad you liked it. I've had some practice."

"Lots of practice?"

She leaned in close and dropped her voice. "It's a highly protected female secret—if you ever reveal this to anyone, I'll have to kill you—but we actually take secret lessons on how to fake it."

A laugh erupted from Griffin. "You must have learned from a master."

She sat back in her seat again and smiled. "If you ever need lessons…"

"Guys don't fake it."

"Oh, come on, don't tell me you haven't had to do it at least once."

"Never."

A flight attendant was prepping the plane for takeoff now, hurrying around and slamming doors. Another flight attendant was collecting drink glasses from the first-class passengers.

Macy eyed him curiously. "Have you ever been to Vegas before?"

"Of course. Who hasn't?"

"*I* haven't," she said.

"Get out of here."

She shrugged. "I'm not even sure I'll know how to debauch myself properly."

"Honey, you just leave me in charge of debauchery, and you'll have no problems."

If only…

If only she'd take him up on his offer. If only she'd give him half a chance to show her what debauchery was all about. He'd be a happy, happy man.

"I hope Carson makes it on the next flight," she said, glancing at her watch. "If this one gets any more delayed, he'll get to Vegas before us."

"Frankly," Griffin said. "I don't give a damn if Carson makes it or not."

"Oh?" She cast a loaded glance at Griffin, and he watched her, wondering what the hell it meant. "Too bad we don't have the weekend alone together," she said, then reopened her steamy novel and started reading again.

Whoa, mama. Back up. "What's that supposed to mean?"

The corner of her mouth twitched, but she kept her gaze on the pages of the book. "Oh, nothing."

Suddenly the canned air blasting out of the little fan above drove Griffin crazy, and he reached up to turn it off. The sound of the plane's engines became louder, and the flight attendant started going through her safety briefing.

He leaned over and snatched the book out of Macy's hands. "Don't you 'oh, nothing' me. I've seen your acting abilities, and impressive as they may be, I know the score now. You can't fool me."

She made a show of stretching, probably all for his benefit. The movement emphasized her full chest, which he could barely tear his gaze away from. Crazy how when he got near her, he could hardly think of her as anything but a collection of irresistible body parts, a being created to torture him with temptation.

"You've got me," she finally said. "I guess I'd better just tell you the deal straight-up."

"That would be a nice change." Wandering into O'Shaunnessy's the other night had been a stroke of pure luck that he'd never be able to thank Carson enough for.

"I just think, if we're going to be in Sin City, anyway..." She smiled and shrugged.

"Go on."

"We ought to take advantage."

"I'm going to need specifics," he said, forcing his tone to stay casual.

She crossed her leg toward him and angled her torso in close. "You, me and a hotel room. No faking it. Is that specific enough?"

Her voice had taken on a sensual quality that left no room for doubting her meaning. If Griffin had been a guy on the cover of a romance novel, he was pretty sure this was the part where he was supposed to take the woman in his arms, rip her dress and start showering her with hungry kisses.

Instead, he cast a glance down at Macy's lace top and wondered how hard a tug it would really take to remove it. Definitely not a maneuver he'd attempt on an airplane.

"No faking it," he said, his mouth suddenly dry, his entire body tensed. Definitely specific enough, and the best idea he'd heard in years.

WHAT HAPPENS in Vegas stays in Vegas.

It was a piece of marketing genius, that slogan. Macy couldn't get it out of her head, not on the plane ride, not in the cab and not now, when it threatened to make her as tipsy as if it were a strong drink.

She looked up at the towering facade of the Golden Gate Resort and Casino—a massive gold building gleaming in the waning sunlight, its style both vaguely art deco and a tribute to the old-style hotels with their neon lights and lack of architectural gizmos—and sighed at the sheer grandness of it all. Speakers discreetly hidden around the hotel grounds played Frank Sinatra music, and if Macy had been wearing a flouncy dress, she wouldn't have been able to resist the urge to do a little spin right there on the sidewalk.

The casino had wanted a San Francisco advertising firm so that they'd have locals who really knew the city helping them recreate the magic of it through advertising. No small task, but something Macy was sure they could handle.

The dry desert wind whipped at her hair, and the heat forced her to remove her blazer before she'd made it halfway up the casino walk.

She was still feeling giddy from her proposition to Griffin on the plane—and his obvious excitement over it. He'd fallen for her act without a hitch, even with the problem of his having seen her in the orgasm contest.

Macy still wasn't sure how she'd get around that little issue, but she figured most guys were so distracted in the final throes of passion that he wouldn't notice a bit of acting on her part. He might wonder afterward, but during? No way.

Griffin had spent half the flight talking about the casino ad campaign. He'd even kept talking after Macy had started reading her book again. The only thing that had gotten him to shut up was when she started reading the steamy parts of her book to him. Nothing like sex to shut a guy up.

And now here they were. Macy hurried in her high-heeled sandals to keep up with Griffin, while he looked around, peering up and down the strip as he walked.

"Great location," he said. "We're right in the middle of it all."

Macy felt a little too overwhelmed by all the sights and sounds to take it in at once. First she needed to get rid of her luggage and the stiff suit she always felt compelled to wear when flying first class, then she'd be ready to check out the casino and the town.

Fifteen minutes later, they'd registered, wandered the gigantic hotel and found their side-by-side rooms. Only when they were standing outside their doors trying to get the damn credit card keys to work did it strike Macy how close she was to completing the first step of her crazy plan.

Suddenly, her stomach revolted and she nearly lost her airplane snack all over the door. "I'll ring you when I'm changed and ready to go out," she called as she hurried inside her room before he could get any ideas.

Just as she closed the door, she caught Griffin's perplexed look and offered him a little wave goodbye. Once she'd closed it, she leaned against it and expelled a ragged breath.

"Damn it."

If she was going to do this, she had to do it right. No freaking out, no throwing up, no turning into a wimp. She took a few deep, cleansing breaths.

Then she noticed her suite. It was amazing. Probably bigger than her apartment in San Francisco—no, definitely bigger, she realized as she wandered from the entryway to the living room. And the view— wow. She opened a balcony door and stepped outside to a panoramic, sparkling, glittering view of the Las Vegas strip.

Down below was a replica of the Golden Gate Bridge and San Francisco Bay, where tourists were taking boat rides around the faux cityscape.

From the next balcony, someone cleared his throat, and she looked over to see Griffin watching her. He smiled. "Pretty amazing, huh?"

"I may never leave this suite," she said.

His gaze traveled over her. "Want to order room service?"

"No way. I lied," she said. "I've gotta leave long enough to check out Las Vegas. After I do that, *then* I'm never leaving this suite."

He leaned against the railing and pinned her with a blatantly sensual gaze. "As long as you don't change your mind, I'd say we've got plenty to keep us busy behind closed doors."

Oh, yes, they did. Macy smiled. "I won't change my mind."

"I'm going to clean up," he said. "See you in a few." And he disappeared behind the dividing wall and into his room.

She needed a little pep talk, Macy decided. She went back inside and dialed Lauren's number, then spilled the details of her so-called evil plan.

"I'm impressed," Lauren said when she'd finished. "You really took my idea to heart."

"Impressed enough to help me?"

Lauren laughed. "Let me guess—you need a distraction for that Carson guy."

"He's cute," Macy said. "Very cute."

"You've got room in your suite for me?"

"I've got room in my suite for a football team."

Silence on the line, while Lauren was probably trying to decide whether Macy was exaggerating Carson's physical appeal.

"Please, please, please, please?"

"Okay, fine, just stop groveling."

"Look at it as your contribution to my career. If it weren't for your study, I wouldn't even be doing this."

"Yeah, yeah. I'll catch the late flight and call your cell phone when I get to the hotel, okay?"

"You're a goddess!"

After she'd hung up, Macy sank onto a brown leather sofa and surveyed her new kingdom. Luxurious gold, red and brown textiles and woods were used throughout the suite. A plasma TV sat on a reproduction art-deco cabinet, and across the room, a bed the size of Macy's entire bedroom at home beckoned. It was the perfect locale for her Las Vegas debauchery—or at least Griffin's probably identical bed would be, since Lauren would likely be occupying this one.

Macy had been telling herself all day that her plan for Griffin was strictly a career move, that she'd never have been doing it if it weren't for Lauren's study, and being in Vegas and blah blah blah.

But she realized now it was more than that. She just plain wanted him. She'd wanted him the first time she saw him, she wanted him even when he pissed her off at work and she wanted him now more than ever. He wasn't the kind of guy she dreamed of falling in love with. He wasn't the kind of dark, brooding lone wolf she couldn't get enough of in the romances she read.

No, he was the kind of guy she would have had a huge crush on in high school, the kind she'd outgrown long ago. But maybe this was all a matter of scoring for her inner nerd. Maybe taking care of her adolescent fantasies would allow her to move on and fulfill her adult ones with someone else.

That motivation made this whole no-orgasm thing trickier than ever. Unless he was lousy in bed…

Hey, a girl could always hope.

GRIFFIN AND Macy had gotten the VIP tour of the casino and hotel, had a short meeting with the owners and now they were free to do as they pleased. Griffin was trying hard not to resort to a childish chant of, "Can we do it now, can we do it now, can we do it now?"

But that's pretty much all he could think about.

Sex.

With Macy.

Nearest private location.

ASAP.

He was like a kid on Christmas Eve and she was the only toy he wanted from Santa. He wasn't going to be satisfied until he had the object of his desire unwrapped and in his hands.

This was yet another example of why they needed to do it and get all the tension out of the air. It couldn't do anything but improve their working relationship for him to get over the idea that one of his coworkers and soon-to-be subordinates was the latest toy he just had to have.

Macy had changed into a clingy little pink dress that was far more appropriate for the hundred-degree June temperature than her suit had been, and Griffin was damn glad of the desert weather. This was the first time he'd ever gotten to see her looking like anything other than a buttoned-up career girl, and as he followed her along the crowded sidewalk on the strip, he couldn't help noticing that she had an even nicer body without all the clothes required by a San Francisco summer.

When Macy spotted the arched walkways of the Venetian, she darted in that direction, and soon they were out of the sidewalk crowds and standing in the shade of the faux Italian corridors.

She looked around and smiled. "If we squint really hard and ignore all the neon lights, we can sort of pretend we're in Italy."

Griffin moved closer to her, and they peered out an arched window at the gondolas floating below. "Have you ever been to Italy?"

She nodded. "I did the college backpacking thing. Slept in grungy hotels, ate cheap pizza, flirted with cheap men. But we never made it to Venice. All my stuff was stolen on a sleeper train and I had to cut my trip short."

"I've been to Venice," he said, smiling at the image of Macy, young and on the loose in Italy. "Lots of pigeons."

"Oh, come on, tell me about it. There has to be more to it than that."

"Okay, there were lots of tourists, too. Sort of like here, but without all the strippers and fast-food restaurants."

She laughed. "I'll be sure and tell Venice not to hire you for their next big ad campaign."

He slid his hand around her waist, savoring the firm, warm feel of her. "Who needs Venice when we've got Vegas, baby?"

He wasn't prepared for how much that simple physical contact would heat him up. And when it was this hot outside, more heat was a dangerous thing.

"I think I've taken care of our Carson problem," Macy said. "I asked a friend of mine to fly out and entertain him while we're, um, otherwise engaged."

An image of Macy's friend at the bar came to mind. But, no, that would have been too sweet a coincidence. "Carson's a big boy. I'm sure he could find plenty to entertain himself with here."

She shrugged. "It's nice to have some company. If they hate each other, no loss. I just thought it might be fun if they hook up."

"Speaking of Carson," Griffin said, pulling his cell phone out of his pocket and checking the time on it, "I wonder if he's checked into the hotel yet."

"Give him a call so we won't look so much like we've completely abandoned him."

Griffin dialed Carson's number and listened as the phone rang twice, then Carson's voice said, "Hello?"

"Hey man, where are you?"

"Still stuck in San Francisco. My flight's delayed but is supposed to leave in a half hour."

"Give me a call when you get in, okay?"

"Got it. Catch you later," Carson said, and Griffin offered a goodbye and clicked off the phone.

A group of tourists wearing matching T-shirts that read Ping-Pong Club of America wandered by, and Griffin caught Macy's amused expression.

"Why aren't there any clubs or T-shirts for the stuff I like to do?" she asked.

"You mean like a fake orgasm club?" he asked, citing the only activity he'd ever seen her participate in outside of work.

She elbowed him in the ribs.

"Ouch!"

"I mean, what is it about Ping-Pong, and not, say, sleeping late on Sundays, that makes people don a T-shirt about it?"

"I'm not even going to touch that question, but please tell me you have some other interest besides sleeping."

"Work hard, sleep hard—that's my philosophy," she said with a self-deprecating smile.

"Don't you have any hobbies? Sports you like to play?"

A gust of wind whipped through the corridor, sending Macy's dress billowing up around her hips. He caught a glimpse of white lace panties, and his cock stirred.

God, he loved the desert. Heat, wind, big hotel suites—what more could a guy ask for?

"Full-contact shopping," she said in answer to his question, once she'd gotten her dress under control. "It's both a hobby and a sport."

But witty as her answer was, Griffin had lost all interest in chitchat now. He couldn't have cared if she liked to knit little hats and scarves for lawn gnomes. He wanted to sleep with her, sooner rather than later. He wanted a closer look at those white lace panties, and what lay beneath the white lace panties—not just a look, but a full-on tour and an invitation to stay a while.

He pulled her against him and let her feel his erection pressing against her abdomen.

"You'll have to teach me about this shopping thing. Later," he said as he slid his hand up her ribcage, over the soft fullness of her breast, along her neck, and into her hair. Just the way her own hand had traveled Wednesday night at the pub.

Her hair felt like fine silk, and as she gazed up at him, he saw for the first time a look of uncertainty. "Are you okay?"

A slow smile curved her lips, and the uncertainty

was gone. "Definitely okay. What about you?" she asked, staring at his mouth. "What's your hobby?"

"It's full-contact," he whispered, dipping his mouth down to taste the delicate edge of her ear. "But not a large group activity, though some people try to make it one."

He covered her mouth with his, and all the air whooshed out of his lungs. She tasted like nothing he could name, but definitely better than cotton candy. Better than any childhood treat he could have imagined.

She moaned and danced her tongue into his mouth, sending a little shock wave through him as she pressed his hips against hers, pinned him to the stone wall.

So this is what it was like to kiss Macy. He finally knew. But there was so much more to know, and what seemed like so little time.

She broke the kiss, and suddenly his mouth felt naked. "This hobby of yours—two people can do it together?"

"That's the best way," he whispered, marveling at how her soft brown eyes resembled chocolate.

He felt crazy, giddy, on a jittery sugar high. Like the first kid ever to taste candy.

Like he'd finally gotten his hands on the toy of his dreams.

And he wanted more.

"I think I'll need a hands-on demonstration," she whispered, and he reclaimed her mouth, took another taste, wondered if he'd ever get enough.

4

MACY WAS not at all prepared for the way it felt to kiss Griffin. She was attracted to him, sure. But she hadn't imagined how contact with him could set her every nerve on fire.

His lips on hers, his hard body against her, his tongue coaxing her into opening up to him even more—it was scorching. It was sensory overload.

She moaned into his mouth, and the sound reminded her that they were in public. She backed off, reluctantly broke the kiss and put a few discreet inches of distance between them. Griffin kept his arms around her, not letting her get too far away.

"Sorry, guess I got a little carried away."

"You and me both," she said, smiling.

"You've got lipstick everywhere," he said as he rubbed his thumb against her chin.

"So do you."

She found a tissue in her purse, along with a compact, and they took turns removing all-day-wear hot pink from themselves.

"Want to walk a little farther down the strip?" Griffin asked.

Macy eyed the hordes of people crowding the sidewalks, and the long line of traffic backed up in each direction. She knew Las Vegas was a popular weekend destination, but wow. It was like Mardi Gras without the parade. No, the casinos were the parade.

But as with everything else this weekend, she decided her policy should be to dive in head-first. "Sure, why not?"

They walked back out to the sidewalk and joined the throng of people, took in the sights, gawked at the whole spectacle. When Griffin took Macy's hand in his, her first instinct was to pull it away—he was her coworker, after all. And her biggest rival, too.

But that didn't exactly make sense if she planned to sleep with him in a matter of hours. And she did, didn't she?

Yes, she did.

She took a deep breath and banished all the niggling doubts that had her on edge.

She was in Sin City, and she wanted more than anything to let the town live up to its reputation. She wanted to have a weekend worthy of such a place, if that made any sense.

"We could catch a show," Griffin was saying, and Macy wondered what else she'd missed while she'd been spacing out.

"Catch a show? Now?"

He gave her a look. "Have you been ignoring me again?"

She felt her face warming, and it had nothing to do with the heat outside. "Um…"

"How are we going to work together if you think nothing I say is important?"

"That's not what I think at all. I'm sorry—I was just so busy looking at everything, I didn't hear you."

"But this happens a lot—you tuning me out."

"It's just that, well, you seem always to be so convinced that you're right, you don't want to hear anyone else's opinion. And I guess I feel like, if my opinion doesn't matter to you, then why should yours matter to me?"

Okay, so this wasn't exactly foreplay talk. But if he wanted the truth, she'd give him the truth.

He stared at her, stunned for a moment. "Is that really how I act? Like I'm always right?"

"Pretty much, yeah. Right now is a rare exception."

"You must think I'm a total jerk."

Uh, yeah. A sexy-as-hell jerk, but still a jerk.

"No," she lied. "I just think you're maybe a bit arrogant, that's all."

They reached a crosswalk and stopped to wait for the light to change. About thirty other people were already crowded around also waiting. Macy peered up at a giant flashing video screen advertising a show where almost everyone looked naked.

Griffin followed her gaze. "Looks interesting."

"I guess if you like naked people, definitely."

"Does anyone not like nakedness?"

"I hear it's pretty unpopular in certain circles, but I, frankly, am all for it when done appropriately."

"Define appropriate." His smile betrayed his confused tone.

"You know. Not at weddings, not at the post office, not in a Speedo if you're sixty years old—that sort of thing."

"Got it. Doubt you'd find anyone to disagree with those rules."

"Well, talk to the retirees wearing Speedos."

"You want to catch a show after dinner?"

"I was thinking maybe we should see the one playing at the Golden Gate, since, you know, we're actually supposed to be working on their campaign and all."

"True. Do you even remember what their show is?"

The light changed, and the mob of people crossed the street with Macy and Griffin in the middle of the pack. The hotel on the next corner had rock music blasting from speakers hidden somewhere, and Macy waited until they'd passed before she spoke again.

As they walked, she noticed there were no birds around. Not a single one. In spite of the fact that there were trees and water fountains everywhere.

"Isn't it kind of weird that there aren't any birds here?" she asked when they'd cleared the loud music.

"I didn't notice," he said, looking around. "But now that you mention it…"

"Maybe they have snipers on the hotel rooftops, shooting any flying creature that enters Las Vegas airspace and threatens to piss off the tourists who then might not want to gamble."

"And maybe there are guys up there with nets, too, to catch the bird carcasses before they hit the ground."

Macy winced at the image, then relaxed into Griffin's

side as he put his arm around her to steer her away from a discarded hot dog on the ground. She hadn't expected to feel so at ease around him when they were away from work. Or to like his off-the-clock personality, which wasn't nearly so cutthroat competitive and aren't-I-great cocky.

"You're kind of sick, you know."

"You started it with the snipers."

Scary how they had such similar senses of humor. Macy rarely met guys who could not only laugh at her jokes, but could join in and do her one better.

"We seriously have to investigate this no-bird phenomenon. Maybe we could use it in the ad campaign—Come to Las Vegas, where no birds will crap on your head."

"Or…Las Vegas—the town where nature will never interfere with your vacation."

"This is great stuff. We should be writing it down."

"I've got a voice recorder in my pocket," Griffin offered.

"Hmm, maybe on second thought…"

"You never answered me about the Golden Gate's show. Any idea what it is?"

"Oh, sorry, I got distracted by the hordes of tourists. I think there's a couple of shows. There's that weird show with all the half-naked people wearing body paint and tap-dancing, and then they have a late-night adults-only show with what we can only assume are lots of dancing people in various stages of undress."

"Sounds like the show for me. But if it's very late—"

"I may be otherwise engaged."

"Just you?" he said, one eyebrow cocked.

"Okay—we may be otherwise engaged. Happy now?"

"Extremely."

With all their talking, Macy hadn't been paying much attention to where they were going, and only now she realized that they'd managed to get themselves up onto a walkway that crossed over the strip.

"Do we have any idea where we're headed?" she asked.

Griffin pointed to a huge hotel with a lake in front of it. "The Bellagio is over there. I figured we'd try to catch one of the fountain shows."

"I'm getting hungry. Feel like grabbing some dinner?"

"I know a place inside the Bellagio. Unbelievable fondue. Sound good?"

"Perfect," she said.

They smiled at each other kind of goofily, and suddenly they were locked in one of those movie moments when time stands still and the audience knows that there's a big shift occurring in the relationship. They were going from competitive coworkers scrambling to get the same promotion, to star-crossed lovebirds sadly doomed to a failed relationship—only they don't know it yet.

Except, Macy did know it. And she hated that she knew it. And she wished like hell that she could have had this weekend without the foreknowledge of the train wreck to come.

GRIFFIN WASN'T normally a fondue kind of guy, but there was something about eating food on a stick with a woman that was distinctly erotic. The whole thing had serious foreplay possibilities. Freud probably would have had a field day with the concept, but hey.

They wandered through the casino, relying on Griffin's shaky memory of the restaurant's location. Around them, the din of slot machines dinging and whirring combined with the smoke in the air and the passing scantily-clad cocktail waitresses had Griffin feeling as though he was doing something slightly scandalous, which only heightened his arousal.

That damn kiss had left him nearly insane with wanting Macy. What was he going to do when they had to work together again come Monday? Drag her to the nearest bathroom stall and have sleazy public-restroom sex?

Even that thought turned him on. He was a basket case.

Macy tugged him toward a row of slot machines. "I've got some extra quarters to blow," she said. "I'm getting tired and thirsty. Let's take a break and buy a drink."

She sat down at a machine and Griffin sat at the one next to her.

"I think this is why they make the restaurants hard to find—so you'll get lost and end up gambling instead."

"Clearly it's an excellent strategy," she said as she fed a quarter into her machine.

Griffin spotted a waitress and waved her over. "What would you like to drink?" he asked Macy.

"A cosmopolitan might quench my thirst," she said

as her slot machine whirred and stopped on a losing spread.

He placed their order with the waitress, then turned and watched Macy continue to feed quarters into the slot.

"You're not having much luck," he said after her tenth or eleventh loss.

"I don't really believe in luck. So probably I shouldn't be gambling. I just wanted to try it once."

"You've never gambled before?"

"You just watched me lose my virginity," she said. "Should I feel honored?"

"Not yet." A little smile played on her lips, and Griffin remembered again why she drove him so crazy at work.

She was the perfect ingenue. So seemingly sweet and guileless, but just beneath the surface lurked a woman who wielded her feminine charms like a deadly weapon.

It took little more than a look, a smile, the slightest gesture, and he could have his entire train of thought wiped away, replaced by fantasies of her and him and a lot of sweaty sex.

She turned her attention back to the machine. "I've got five more quarters. The odds are in favor of my winning something soon, right?"

"If it's all about the odds and not luck, I'd say the best you can hope for is getting your quarters back."

"Oh ye of little faith."

Another quarter in the slot, and the cherries all lined up. The machine lit up, and fifty quarters came dinging out.

"See," Macy said. "It's not luck. It's just odds. And I didn't win much—further proof that no luck was involved."

"Hey, I'm not arguing with you. Most people's seeming luck is hard work and planning, but you can't spend any time on a sports field without knowing that sometimes luck enters into it."

"You still play any sports?" Macy asked.

The waitress arrived, gave them their drinks and Griffin paid her.

"I play softball, basketball, soccer, the occasional round of golf, volleyball—"

"Okay, okay, you still play sports."

She had to have heard of his athletic abilities around the office, where he'd pretty much dominated everyone who'd challenged him to a match of anything after work hours.

"How about you?"

"I'm not very coordinated, and I'm afraid of balls."

He tried not to laugh.

"The big ones that come careening toward my head during athletic events, I mean."

"Absolutely. I wasn't thinking anything else."

She rolled her eyes and started gathering her tokens up in a plastic cup that had been sitting beside the machine.

"So what do you do to stay in such great shape?"

"Kickboxing aerobics classes twice a week and Budokon twice a week. Plus roller-skating on Sundays."

"What's Budokon?"

"It combines martial arts, yoga and meditation. Sounds weird, but it's actually very cool."

Griffin was trying not to be impressed, but he was. For a girly girl, she had a pretty kick-butt workout routine. And he had a weakness for women who stayed in shape.

"And you go roller-skating? Like at a roller rink?"

"No, at Golden Gate Park. Sunday afternoons it's the happening place to be. And it makes me feel like a kid again, except without all the misery and angst."

"I can't believe you were a miserable kid."

"Believe it. If you knew my mother, you'd see why."

"What's with all the aggressive aerobic workouts?" he asked, then downed a good long swallow of his Heineken, trying not to get a boner from the image of Macy dressed in skimpy workout clothes, sweaty and practicing kicking ass.

"I've got lots of pent-up rage, I guess," she said with a self-deprecating smile.

"From?"

"Maybe from the aforementioned mother—I don't know. Or maybe from being the biggest nerd in school and never having the guts to stand up for myself."

"There's no way you were a nerd."

"Oh, yes, there is." She finished gathering her tokens, then polished off her cosmo in one long drink. "Let's go cash these in," she said.

Griffin followed her to the cashier's counter, and once Macy had collected her money, they got directions to the fondue place and discovered they'd been only one wrong turn from getting there.

The restaurant was sleek and modern, with lots of dark shiny surfaces and low, moody lighting. Each table consisted of a round booth, and a hostess led them to a small one made for two. They slid into the seat, where it was nearly impossible not to touch when sitting together. Knees and hips brushing against each other, Griffin decided this was an even better place to bring a date than he'd remembered.

They checked out the menus, placed their orders, and the waitress quickly came back with a complimentary appetizer cheese fondue and rosemary bread for dipping.

Macy dipped a piece of bread and took a bite. "I could take a bath in this stuff," she said afterward.

"I'd like to watch that."

"You're not about subtlety, are you?"'

"Subtlety's overrated." Griffin took a bite of bread dipped in fondue, but he barely tasted it.

He was too focused on the sight of Macy taking a bite herself, and the way her mouth looked so impossibly erotic with that slightest drip of cheese on her lower lip that she tried and failed to retrieve with a flick of her tongue. His sadly predictable cock stirred, like clockwork, and he shifted to ease the tightness of his pants. But that led to his leg entangling with Macy's, and then he wasn't sure if he wanted to sit through a whole damn dinner suffering this kind of delicious agony.

Couldn't they just go back to the hotel room now and get naked?

Well, he probably wouldn't win any points for

subtlety or class by suggesting it now. But he could hurry things along a little by making sure Macy was suffering the same kind of agony as him. It only seemed fair.

He slipped his hand across her thigh and inadvertently pushed her skirt up. Which left his hand on her bare, silky thigh.

She paused in mid chew and looked at him as though she was amused in either a good way or a bad way by his boldness. When she edged her thigh closer, inviting his hand to go farther up, he had to assume it was the good kind of amusement.

The dim lighting and the mostly enclosed booths gave them just enough privacy that an onlooker would have to be straining pretty hard to see what was going on under the table. Griffin slid his hand a little farther toward heaven; her eyes fluttered shut, and her mouth softened.

Tempting his self-control, he leaned forward and kissed her. His tongue brushed against the drop of cheese on her lip, licked it off, then took the time to explore the rest of her lip's satiny surface. When he summoned all his self-control to pull away, her eyes were still closed.

And when she looked at him again, her sultry brown eyes were clouded with blatant desire, a do-me expression so loud and clear he was surprised other people weren't staring.

But the restaurant was only half-full, and the tables were arranged for maximum privacy so that none of the booth openings faced each other. There really wasn't anyone, other than passersby, who could even stare.

He eased his hand up farther, and his fingertips brushed the warm juncture of her thighs. Her gaze turned daring.

She smiled a secret little smile. "I dare you."

Her thighs parted, and all the blood left his brain. He should have passed out, but being a typical guy he had plenty of experience with blood rushing to his groin, and somehow he managed to remain upright.

Her panties were the silky kind, and they didn't seem to cover much. Griffin slipped his fingers over the top of them, down to where she was hottest, over her clit, and she made a purring sound low in her throat that could have toppled lesser men.

This wasn't the kind of dipping he'd had in mind when he'd suggested they get fondue, but hell, sometimes the best things in life were the unplanned events, the little invitations out of the blue, the secret exchanges under the table.

She picked up another piece of bread and dipped it in the pot of cheese, then offered it to him. He took a bite, keeping his gaze pinned on her, and then she ate the remaining bread slowly as she watched him.

He glided his fingers over her, back and forth, back and forth, watching her melt against the seat. When the waitress arrived and placed their dinner fondue on the table, along with trays of their dipping meats and vegetables, he stilled his hand, and Macy cast him a mock-offended look.

When the waitress left, Macy said, "Why'd you stop?"

"Sorry. I didn't want to get busted and have to try and fit our fondue into carryout containers."

"Yeah, the fire probably wouldn't travel well."

"Or we'd have to extinguish it, and by the time we got to the hotel we'd have blocks of cheese instead of dip."

"I'll feed you if you'll go back to what you started," she whispered as she dipped a carrot stick in fondue and offered it to him.

"That's the best offer I've had in a while," he said, then took a bite as he slipped his fingers under the edge of her panties.

Her eyes fluttered shut again, and she dropped the carrot on a tray. As he glided his fingers between her lips and over her clit, he could see her breath growing shallow, could almost taste her. He slipped a finger inside her, where she was slick and wet, and suddenly the whole idea of eating dinner seemed preposterous.

What the hell had they been thinking? They could have been in a hotel room by now, getting it on while they waited for room service. Screw room service, he didn't really need anything to eat except Macy.

"What do you say we blow this fondue joint?" he asked.

She opened her eyes. "I'm sorry. I'm not doing a very good job of upholding my end of the bargain by feeding you."

"I'm not really interested in eating carrots right now."

She made a sad face. "I ruined dinner for you?"

"I'd rather have you for dinner."

"I really work better as a dessert. And if we leave now, I'll lose my chance to entice you with lots of mouth and tongue work on the carrot sticks."

Griffin smiled at her ability to make fun of herself. But with his finger still inside her, he wasn't really in the mood for conversation. He glided his slick fingertips over her clit, around in circles, slowly, as her eyes took on that glazed look again.

He wanted to make her come right here in the middle of the restaurant. He'd never done anything so public before, aside from a stupid stunt in high school under the football stadium bleachers, but as an adult... Macy wiped away all his reservations, all his common sense and apparently all his fear of being arrested.

She was getting wetter and wetter, and just when he thought she was about to come, she pulled away. Moved her leg, gently removed his hand from her, and made some adjustments to her clothes as she put a discreet distance between them.

She smiled a slow, wicked smile. "I don't want to have dessert first," she said. "Let's save some fun for later."

"I've got all kinds of fun in mind for later. I thought that was just an appetizer."

The tightened coil inside him loosened, and while his cock was still hard, he could feel some of his sense coming back to him. Okay, he could wait. He could play the respectable guy, sit here and eat dinner, delay gratification.

No problem.

"We can't let all this fondue go to waste, I guess."

She picked up a piece of salami, dipped it and took a bite. He stared at her mouth again, mesmerized.

Sure, he could make it through dinner. He might

have to go to the bathroom and hammer some nails into the wall with his erection, but he could make it no problem.

5

WHEN THE waitress asked about dessert, Macy could only think of obscene things to do with melted chocolate. Turned out, the restaurant had a fondue-to-go container that kept the stuff hot for up to three hours, and with that news Macy and Griffin had promptly placed an order for chocolate and strawberries to go.

She would never be able to think of dipping fondue the same way again. And she had no idea how she'd survive the rest of the night, let alone the rest of the weekend, without coming.

Okay, so Griffin could be an arrogant jerk at work. She had to focus on that. She had to remember that he was the kind of handsome jock who'd alternately ignored her and made fun of her in high school. She had to remember that this was revenge of the nerd. It wasn't about getting her groove on. It was about getting even, and getting Griffin dumbed down for his Monday presentation.

By the time they made it to the hotel elevator, there was no longer any room for pretending that they cared about making a spectacle in public.

When the elevator dropped off the only other couple

on board on the third floor and they were alone, Griffin dropped the bag of dessert on the floor and pinned Macy against the elevator wall. He devoured her in an urgent kiss, and the feel of his erection thrilled her for all the wrong reasons. She should have been excited that her plan was working so far, but instead she could only think of finally having Griffin inside her.

Finally having him.

His hands grazed her breasts and her traitorous rock-hard nipples, and his tongue teased hers. He tasted vaguely like beer, and he felt exactly like heaven.

But why was she so thrilled to have him? Was this really revenge of the nerd if the nerd so lacked self-respect that she was still thrilled to have the attention of Mr. Popularity?

God, she was pitiful.

She summoned all her strength and pulled away, gently urging his hands off her, then slipping out from between him and the elevator wall.

"I forgot, security cameras," she said, nodding at the one in the corner. "Wouldn't want some bubba to get off watching us."

Griffin smiled. "So now you're being modest?"

"There weren't any cameras under the table at the restaurant. Or at least I hope there weren't."

The elevator stopped, Griffin retrieved dessert from the floor, and they got out. They walked down the hallway toward their suites holding hands.

"Your place or mine?" he asked.

"I'm waiting to hear from my friend Lauren, so my place."

Macy tried to psych herself into being detached from this whole sexing up Griffin thing, but she couldn't get past actually being attracted to him. This was all wrong. She wasn't supposed to fall for the big jerk-ass. But then again, he wasn't acting like a big jerk-ass, and she was just confused as hell.

"Something wrong?" Griffin asked. "You seem like something upset you in the elevator."

And for a jerk-ass, he was surprisingly perceptive. How come he never managed to pick up on her feelings at work? Or maybe he did, but didn't think they mattered when it came to business....

Dear God, she was confused.

"No, I mean. Well, maybe. I guess I'm just freaking out a little."

"Because?"

"Up until today, we were just two people who worked together and didn't get along especially well."

"Sexual tension. It can wreak havoc in the workplace. So we're actually doing each other a favor by diffusing it."

Um, right.

"I guess you're right. I just never imagined acting on our attraction, you know."

"No, I don't know. I've spent lots of time imagining it."

He had?

Well, truthfully, so had she, but no way was she going to admit it. Instead, she flashed a smile. "Fantasies are one thing. Acting them out can have unintended consequences."

They reached her room, and before she could find her security card, he had her wedged against the door, his mouth inches from hers. This was one time when his aggressiveness was much appreciated. Even if she wasn't supposed to be appreciating it, she couldn't help herself.

"Tonight," he said, their lips nearly touching now. "I say, forget the consequences."

Macy's insides melted. She was a silly fool. A girl who'd been deprived of so much handsome jock attention that she didn't know how to handle it now that she could get it.

But the consequences were exactly why she was doing this, right? Let him forget them, but she had to keep them in the forefront of her mind all night.

And as long as she could do that, she'd be okay. She tilted her chin, and their lips met. She'd meant it to be a soft kiss, but there didn't seem to be any slow setting on their attraction. Suddenly they were locked in a kiss that was all searching tongues and throaty moans, all grinding hips and wandering hands.

It was nice to be this wanted. It really was.

Stupid. Stupid thoughts again. Macy somehow untangled herself from Griffin long enough to find her card, unlock the door and step into the foyer. But they didn't make it very far.

The door slammed shut, and inside the room, a nightstand lamp was on, bathing the room in a soft yellow glow. Perfect lighting for sex. Not harsh enough to highlight many flaws, but just enough light to enhance the show.

Somehow the bed seemed too far away. Macy dropped her purse, Griffin dropped dessert again, and she couldn't reconstruct in her head how they ended up on the foyer floor. She was pretty sure she'd fallen down, but then Griffin was pushing her dress strap off her shoulder and licking her nipple and she really couldn't manage to give a damn how they'd gotten there or whether they'd ever leave it.

Now he had both breasts exposed, and Macy arched her back, pressing herself toward him as delicious tension built up inside her. She heard herself moaning; her fingers were tangled in his hair, and she had no idea where all this crazy desire had come from. When his fingers made their way to her panties again, she thought she might cry.

To have all this pleasure and not be able to take it to its natural conclusion—it wasn't going to be easy.

He pushed her panties down, plunged his fingers into her, massaged and coaxed her toward the one place she wasn't supposed to go.

Maybe she could spare a few IQ points…

Just a couple of little ones

Like the ones she used for remembering useless dates or names of people she no longer knew.

Her dress was bunched around her waist now, and Griffin was exploring lower and lower with his tongue. This was where she was supposed to turn the tables, distract him, something.

She definitely shouldn't have let him go where he was going. But, oh, she just wanted to feel his tongue there for a second, for a minute…

Five minutes max.

And then she'd definitely put a stop to it.

Abso-freaking-lutely.

His tongue flicked against her clit, and she sighed. He began sucking and probing and working all sorts of magic, and then Macy was making some crazy gasping sounds, as if she'd just run a marathon or something. She spread her legs wide, lifted herself to his mouth, ground against him. Wanted more of him.

Thank goodness there was finally a conviction she could get behind.

"I want you inside me," she said.

But he didn't stop.

"Please," she begged, tugging at his hair a tiny bit and attempting to wriggle away.

He held her hips still, and Macy wasn't quite as behind her newfound conviction as she intended to be. She collapsed on the floor and closed her eyes, swept away by the delicious rhythm of his tongue.

But she was getting perilously close to having an orgasm. She could feel the delicious tension building, the heaviness in her groin, and she had to stop it.

No, no, no, no, no.

She couldn't let it happen.

She summoned all her strength, wriggled away again, sat up and started undressing him.

His gaze, half-lidded, warmed her. He was taking in the sight of her naked, and Macy could only hope he liked the view. Even after losing weight in college, she'd stayed curvy, and men had never made a secret of loving her full breasts.

The rest of her body, well, she wasn't exactly Kate Moss, but then no one ever complained. And she was too damn happy to be healthy to nitpick herself. She looked good enough. Hell, in dim light, she looked fantastic.

And so did Griffin. She'd freed him of his shirt, and now he was taking off his shoes...his pants...his boxers. He had a stunning athlete's body, still hard and trim, all sculpted muscle, not gone to flab the way so many guys did after their glorious youth. For that, she had to give him his props.

His eyes were still locked on her, and she didn't try to hide her staring at him. She let her gaze travel over him slowly, and his large, full cock deserved special attention.

Heaven help her. She was a believer that size did matter, and it was going to matter more than ever tonight.

Here was hoping he didn't know how to drive that big rig with any kind of expertise.

GRIFFIN WANTED to finish what he'd started. He didn't like being known as a one-hit wonder in bed, and he took pride in making sure his lovers came many times during an encounter. Once was never enough, not for him, and definitely not for the women he slept with.

"You should have let me finish," he said. "I like to think I'm pretty good at it—"

"Oh, you are," Macy said, and then she kissed him.

Her hand gripped his cock, and they were on their knees now, face-to-face. He intended that they should make it to the bed, or at the very least a solid piece of furniture to avoid rug burns, but then he was on his back and she was straddling his hips and all he could think to say was, "There's a condom in my wallet."

She found it, opened the wrapper, put it on him, and he was too hypnotized by the sway of her ridiculously perfect breasts to do anything. He was normally more of a leg man than a breast man, but Macy had just converted him. He was a believer now.

Hallelujah.

He loved their weight, the way they moved, and when he thrust into her, the way they bounced. As her hot, tight opening took him in, he couldn't imagine which was more perfect—her pussy or her tits.

No, all of her.

She was perfect, from her soft, pretty face to the slight curve of her belly, from her lush pink nipples to her long, narrow legs, she was freaking perfect.

No wonder he had such a hard time working with her.

She began rocking against him, riding him, moving his cock deeper into her, and he could only grip her hips and enjoy the show. Her hair spilled over her eyes, framing her face with a wild mop of waves, and she slid her hands up her torso as she rode him, gliding over her belly, cupping her breasts, teasing her nipples.

Damn he loved watching a woman touch herself. Loved the arousal in her expression, loved her soft gasps and moans.

She quickened her rocking, and he meant to slow her down. He didn't want to come too fast, wanted to savor this, make it last. But then she dropped one hand behind her back and dragged her fingernails gently over his balls, and he was nearly done.

He willed himself not to come, tried to remember that he was supposed to be pleasuring her. Or something like that. She continued to caress him as she rode his cock, and it all became too much.

He had to do something to slow this down, and fast.

She was so much hotter than he'd imagined. Macy showed him the limits of his imagination—in the softness of her skin, in the pleasures of her curves, in the eagerness of her touch.

He sat up, held her tight and lifted her with him as he stood. Against-the-wall sex was the hardest kind, guaranteed to slow them down enough that he could savor this once-in-a-lifetime experience.

He held her weight with his hips. Where their bodies came together, he burned. And when he plunged himself inside her, he gasped with the relief of it.

This woman.

Had there ever been a woman he'd wanted more? Had he ever felt more stripped bare by his desire? As if he could do things that wouldn't otherwise be humanly possible? As if running naked through a blizzard would seem a minor sacrifice if it meant having Macy the way he did right now?

He found her mouth and kissed her. Drank her in. They kissed wild, hungry kisses until they had to come up for air, and then with her breasts against him, with her sweet hot pussy taking in his cock, he never wanted it to stop.

Her thighs holding tight to his hips, he pumped into her again and again, their breath intermingling, their bodies growing damp from their effort.

Macy's face was a picture of desire. He wanted to paint it. To burn it into his memory. He watched her—her eyes closed, her brow slightly furrowed, her mouth soft and full—and he memorized it all.

His legs began to shake under the effort of their sex, and he knew he couldn't hold out much longer. He felt an impossible tightness growing inside him. Pleasure coiled tighter and tighter, and there was no stopping.

Lifting her again, he eased them both onto the floor, where she straddled his waist, and he rested on his elbows for those final delicious thrusts.

He bucked against her, cried out, felt his come shoot into her, lost himself in the pulsing frenzy of pleasure. Aftershocks rocked him as she dipped her head and laid claim to his mouth. And somewhere in their kissing, he managed to catch his breath.

Only then did it occur to him that she hadn't come yet.

Oops.

He pulled her down on top of him, his cock still deep inside her, and he whispered, "That wasn't supposed to happen so fast, or without you."

She giggled. "Sorry. Guess we got a little carried away."

"Why don't we move this all the way into the room and do it right?"

"We were doing it wrong?" she asked, feigning confusion.

Griffin eased out of her, rolled her off him and removed the condom. He went into the bathroom and dropped it into the garbage. Back out again, he offered Macy a hand and helped her to a standing position.

"Far as I'm concerned," he said, "anytime my girl doesn't come before me, we're doing something wrong."

"Oh," she said, looking a little…shocked?

Poor thing probably hadn't had a really selfless lover before. And if that was the case, he'd just have to give her an extra dose of selflessness.

"Does that shock you?" he said as he led her to the bed.

"Um, no. I just figure, what does it matter who comes first?"

"It matters because I believe it's incredibly important to pleasure the woman I'm with. It's a measure of my manhood."

She stretched out on the bed on her side, and the sexy curve of her hip nearly did him in. "Isn't that overstating the case. I mean, who's counting?"

"I am," Griffin said. "And I'm starting to get the feeling all the guys you've ever slept with were serious losers in bed."

She shrugged. "I've done all right."

"No one should ever have to describe their sex life as 'all right,' don't you think?"

A smile played on her lips. She appeared to be considering it. "I guess I'm more interested in the connection, the whole experience. It's not all about the grand finale to me."

Something about her words rang false, but Griffin

wasn't exactly in a state to give the matter any deep thought. A little bit of foreplay, a lot of pleasure for her, and he'd be ready to rock again.

"I know a lot of women think that, but seriously, it's just a symptom of having been with lousy lovers. It's like playing the game but not finishing it. Sure, playing the game is fun, but if you don't get through the final round and declare a winner, you've lost the whole point."

"A sports analogy? An orgasm equals winning?" She was looking more amused by the second, and Griffin had a feeling he'd taken a wrong turn somewhere.

Then he remembered the chocolate fondue, and suddenly he knew how to revive the night. He disappeared from the side of the bed and retrieved the dessert bag. He put the container of strawberries and the warm container of chocolate on the nightstand.

"Are you ready for dessert?"

"Now we're talking," she said.

He sat down next to Macy, opened the chocolate, dipped his finger inside, and offered it to her. She took his hand and kept her gaze locked on him as she slowly licked his finger, then sucked it into her mouth.

His erection was already coming back.

Damn, the things they could do with fondue. It boggled the mind. He dipped another finger into the chocolate, withdrew it and traced it over Macy's breast.

"Hey, it works as body paint," she said as she watched.

Griffin bent and licked the chocolate from her. Then he dipped again…painted again…licked again.

"Who needs strawberries when I've got you here?" he asked.

She stretched to grab a strawberry, dipped it in chocolate, then took a bite. Dipped it again, then offered a bite to him. "I think the strawberries could still come in handy," she said.

He took a bite. Shook his head. "No, you definitely taste better."

And with that he went back to licking the last traces of chocolate from her breasts and belly. Once he'd finished, he moved lower again, plunging his tongue into her pussy until she was squirming and crying out his name.

He coaxed her closer and closer to the finish line, making every oral-sex move he knew.

He prided himself on reading a woman's signs. He knew all the stages leading up to orgasm. The calm before the storm, the build-up, the tensing muscles, the release, the waves of pleasure.

But Macy, oddly, wasn't showing the usual signs.

So when she suddenly tensed and cried out in desperate, throaty gasps, he had to wonder...

Was she faking it?

He tried to recall the way she'd sounded in the fake orgasm contest. Different from now, he was pretty sure, but his cock was rock-hard now, and he couldn't think very coherently.

No, couldn't be fake.

But his fingers were inside her, his tongue against her clit. It wasn't as erect as it should have been. And there were no contracting muscles inside her. Something wasn't quite right.

Why the hell would she fake it?

But, maybe he was just too crazed. He probably wasn't reading the signs.

When she'd recovered, he lay down beside her and draped his arm over her belly. "Did you just fake it?"

Her eyes shot open. "Of course not. Why would you say that?"

She sounded thoroughly offended by the suggestion, and the last thing he wanted to do right now was piss her off.

"I don't know. I'm sorry—guess I'm just overly suspicious after that contest the other night."

She expelled a sigh. "Oh. That. Forget it. I was just acting on a stupid dare."

"Promise?"

She kissed him long and slow, her hand finding his cock and massaging all the right spots. "I promise," she whispered against his lips.

That was all the convincing he needed.

6

MACY STRETCHED OUT beside Griffin after they finished
making love. She wanted more than anything to let
them have another go at it, but if they did, she doubted
she could hold back. Well, maybe she could, but she'd
need some time to give herself another pep talk first.

She had to keep in mind that this was all about
dumbing down Griffin, and not at all about her own
sexual pleasure.

But damn it, he'd tried so hard. And he'd gotten so
close to making her come.

She traced her fingers along his ribcage, and he
jerked, swatting her hand away. "That tickles," he said.

"Poor baby."

He rolled over onto her, pinning her to the bed.
"Let's see how you like it then," he said as he began
poking her ribs.

She laughed and squirmed, fighting to get his hands
away but failing.

The phone rang, and Macy realized just how late it
was. Late enough for Lauren to have arrived.

"Hello," she answered, breathless from their wres-
tling.

"Um, did I interrupt something?" Lauren asked, sounding more than a little suspicious.

"No, I was just...running from the bathroom."

"Was it chasing you?"

"What?"

"Never mind," Lauren said. "I'm here. I'm tired. I want a bed to sleep in."

"My room is 2218. Come on up," she said, flashing a warning look at Griffin.

He snapped to attention, sitting up and looking at her in alarm. When Macy hung up the phone, she hopped off the bed and went to look for her clothes.

"Lauren's here. You've got to vacate the premises pronto."

"Just me? Aren't you going to come over and keep me company tonight?"

He managed to look so puppy-dog pitiful, even with his bare, bulging pecs and his rippling abs on display, that Macy couldn't have imagined turning him down even if she hadn't had an ulterior motive.

"I've got to stay here to open the door for Lauren and give her a key, and then I'll come over. Happy?"

"I will be when I've got you in my bed," he said, tugging on his pants. "And don't spend too long chit-chatting. I want you over there before I fall asleep waiting for you."

"Yes, sir."

Macy watched as he did a half-assed dressing job, grabbed his shoes and socks, and left her room to go next door. When he was gone, she heaved a gigantic sigh of relief.

Or was it relief? Maybe it was more like a release of tension—all the tension that was building up inside her as she tried not to be on the receiving end of Griffin's considerable pleasure-giving abilities.

She finished getting herself dressed, debating how much she wanted to tell Lauren about what had already gone down tonight. She normally wasn't a kiss-and-tell kind of girl, but these were special circumstances. And Lauren was a scientist. Maybe she would have some kind of medically sound tips on how to have sex without enjoying it too much.

She straightened up the covers on the bed so that it didn't appear as though anyone had been on it, and she went to the bathroom and grabbed a bottle of hairspray to spray in the air to cover up any lingering sex odors.

Not that she could smell anything. But Lauren had a bizarrely acute sense of smell. She was like a dog the way she went around noticing scents that no ordinary human could detect.

Macy had just finished spraying when there was a knock at the door. She opened the door to her friend and smiled.

"I owe you big-time."

"Yes, you do," Lauren said as she breezed past pulling a small rolling suitcase, with a leopard-print carry-on bag slung over one arm. "I had to sit next to a guy on the plane who spent an hour telling me about how he engineers plastic tubes for a living."

"On the bright side, now you're in Vegas. In a kick-ass hotel suite."

Lauren put down her bags on a bench and looked around. "This place rocks."

"Told you."

"Give me the scoop on this Carson guy I'm supposed to be entertaining," Lauren said as she took off her shoes.

"He's hot—about six feet tall, green eyes, medium-brown hair, great body. He's kind of a…" What was the best spin to put on the fact that Carson probably loved sex more than anything else in life?

"A what?"

"A ladies' man."

"So what you're saying is he's a total pussy hound."

Macy winced. Lauren never fell for her advertising slants. She had an uncanny ability to see through bullshit.

"I wouldn't use those words specifically, but he does love the ladies."

"Like to the point of male slutdom, or what?"

"I only know what I hear through the grapevine at work, but…"

"It's okay. I can hang with that. Have condoms, will travel, right?"

"I think you'll like him."

"I just need a willing body this weekend, and it sounds like he'll be that, correct?"

"Most definitely."

Lauren was unpacking her suitcase now, removing outfits she only wore when she was in a serious party mood and hanging them in the closet.

"Okay, so here's my story. I'm a flight attendant

based in San Francisco. I work for United, and I'm not into commitment."

"What are you talking about?"

"I just want a weekend fling, okay? And guys usually don't want to fling with brainiac medical researchers who've just discovered that sex is the root of all idiocy. So let's keep those little details under wraps. Got it?"

"Um, sure, I guess. But I'm really not buying that whole guys-don't-go-for-smart-women thing."

"Is my love life not a cautionary tale about that very issue?"

Macy eyed the impressive array of lingerie Lauren had packed. Carson was going to be one happy boy.

"You know how I feel about that. Your love life is much more likely a cautionary tale about the dangers of being a commitment-phobic man-eater."

"What's that supposed to mean?"

"It means you take what you want from guys, then toss them aside and move on to your next victim."

Lauren shot her a familiar glare. "You make me sound like such a wicked bitch."

"You *are* wicked."

A mysterious smile crossed her friend's lips. "You don't know the half of it."

The phone rang again, and Macy jumped at the sound, then grabbed the receiver.

"Where the hell are you?" Griffin asked when she answered.

"I'll be there in just a few. I promise."

"I'm getting tired. I need stimulation."

"Then turn on some pay-per-view porn or something," Macy said and hung up.

"Porn? Is there something I should know?" Lauren said as she flopped down on the bed still in her street clothes.

"That was Griffin. He's waiting for me in the next room."

"Very interesting." Lauren sat up on one elbow, her perfectly sculpted black eyebrows arching.

"We've already, um, been kind of busy tonight."

"And?"

"And it's freaking torture! I mean, I just want to let go and enjoy it, but you of all people know what happens then."

Lauren smiled. "You start liking Britney Spears and thinking *Married with Children* reruns are high-brow entertainment."

"Exactly."

"Just enjoy yourself until you're about to come. Don't try to ruin the whole experience. You're there— you might as well savor it."

"But if I let myself get all worked up, won't that make it harder not to come?"

"Not at all. Women are hardwired through aeons of lousy lovers to enjoy delayed gratification. We're so used to almost coming, but not having the guy push the right buttons to get the job done, that our bodies have actually adapted to the whole frustrated-sex process and release endorphins that help us enjoy ourselves quite nicely whether or not we actually have an orgasm."

"I can't believe we're having this conversation."

"It's all true."

"So I've actually wasted a potentially enjoyable sexual experience by spending most of the time trying to think about scrubbing my toilet."

"Ew."

"Exactly." Macy grabbed her overnight bag out of the closet, went into the bathroom and tossed a few essentials inside. She grabbed some clean underwear and a change of clothes from the closet and put those in, too.

"Then you'd better go get yourself some endorphins before you explode."

"I'll call you in the morning and let you know where we'll hook up with Carson, okay?"

Lauren lay down flat on the bed again and closed her eyes. "Okay, and remember, I'm a flight attendant!"

MACY TAPPED SOFTLY on Griffin's door and waited. A few moments later, he was there in front of her, undressed again except for a pair of black Calvin Klein boxers that fit him extraordinarily well.

"Got the porn on yet?" she asked as she brushed past him into the room.

"Are you serious?"

"Only when I'm doing my taxes."

He closed the door, then followed her and captured her in his arms from behind. She felt his erection pressing into her backside, and instantly, that familiar burning started inside her again.

"I *was* kind of serious about the porn, though."

"Whatever you want, babe," he whispered against her neck, then kissed her there.

She melted against him as his teeth nipped at the flesh of her neck, her shoulder.

"I've got this thing for cheesy soft-core skin flicks. Is that something I shouldn't ever admit to anyone?"

"Maybe not, but it's kind of hot, too."

"And you can use it against me later if you ever need to blackmail me," she said, her eyes closed, her body all too willing to enjoy the pleasures he offered.

His hands explored up and down, one massaging her breast as the other dipped between her legs.

In truth, she had high hopes that the porn would be a complete turn-off. That way she wouldn't get so damn aroused. It was a shaky plan at best, but she was willing to try anything at this point. She wasn't totally ready to buy into Lauren's endorphins-are-enough theory.

She struggled out of his grasp and went to the armoire that held the entertainment system, grabbed the remote and turned on the TV.

"Hey, come back here," he said, but she evaded his grasp again, giggling as she scrambled across the bed.

A minute later, they were staring at a menu of pay-per-view erotic movies. *More Bounce to the Ounce, Selena's Secrets, Blame It on Vegas* and *High Ballers* were their choices.

"Hmm," Macy said. "What do you think? Anything sound intriguing?"

"Could we pass up the chance to watch a movie called *High Ballers?*"

"I was just thinking the exact same thing."

"Should we bother to read the plot description?"

Macy scrolled to the title and selected it. She read the description aloud. "A horny group of strip-poker players take the game to new levels of erotic pleasure."

"Hmm."

"Sounds straightforward to me."

She used the remote to navigate her way through the warning that Griffin's hotel bill would reflect a charge of $9.95 for the movie.

Griffin crawled across the bed and pulled her down onto him as the movie's opening credits rolled. "I wouldn't have pegged you for a girl who's into porn."

"I'm full of surprises," she whispered right before kissing him.

Why did he have to feel so damn good?

"I noticed," he said when they broke the kiss.

Macy wriggled around until she was resting in the crook of his arm and could see the TV screen, where a guy was playing poker with a table full of chesty babes in skimpy clothes. Within about two minutes, one of them was under the table giving him a blow job, and another was taking off her top because it was, of course, conveniently a strip-poker game.

When the game quickly wrapped up and everyone was on the table having an orgy, Macy bit her lip and tried not to laugh. Laughing might spoil the mood...which probably wasn't such a bad thing on her end. But for Griffin, well, guys apparently weren't so crazy about laughing in bed.

"Is he doing what I think he's doing?" Griffin asked.

Macy twisted her head to the side, trying to view the scene at a better angle. "Yep."

"Wow."

Macy bit her lip with more force.

"I didn't even know that was possible."

"Want to try it?" she asked, inching her hand along his thigh, fully aware that his erection was about to pop out the barn door of his boxers.

"Um, I think a special surgical procedure is required before a guy can comfortably get into that position."

"Oh."

She stared at the screen, mesmerized by all the moving body parts. And in spite of herself, she was getting aroused. Really aroused. So maybe she was a little freakier than she'd given herself credit for.

And this whole not-coming thing was a little more complicated than Macy had anticipated. She could get through it, though. She just needed to stay focused, but the movie wasn't helping.

Maybe if she just got things moving along here in the real world, she'd be able to tune it out. She slid down, trailing kisses over the rugged terrain of Griffin's chest and abdomen, stopping when she reached his boxers. She tugged them off him, and he watched her, his eyes glazed with arousal.

She undressed, doing her best to make a show of it. Judging by Griffin's expression, she did a decent job. She settled between his legs and slowly licked his erection, loving the hot, firm feel of him.

When she took him into her mouth, he gasped, and his fingers dug into the blankets on the bed. She tasted, licked and coaxed him toward another release.

And with the sounds of the movie in the background—even a flick as cheesy as *High Ballers*—Macy felt herself growing more and more excited. She loved the sound of his heavy breathing mingled with the sex sounds coming from the TV, loved the feeling of power that came with bringing him such an intimate kind of pleasure, loved having such a powerful effect on his body.

With her hands and mouth, she brought him closer and closer to the edge, and then they were there. He cried out and strained toward her as he spilled into her mouth. Macy felt herself nearly vibrating with her own arousal as she drank him in until the waves of pleasure had passed.

She crawled on top of him and lay there, listening to his heartbeat and his breathing.

One more orgasm down, countless more to go.

7

SATURDAY MORNING Macy woke up feeling as if she'd run a marathon. Her body ached in odd places, but in a good way. She got up before Griffin, showered and put on her clothes from the night before. She was about to slip out the door to go to her room and get dressed when he stirred.

"Hey, what're you doing out of bed?" he said as he stretched.

"I need to get some clean clothes and catch up with Lauren. And you should probably track down Carson before he thinks we've permanently abandoned him."

"Oh, right. Him. Why don't we all meet up for breakfast downstairs at the buffet in a half hour? Will that work for you?"

"Assuming Lauren's awake and ready to go, yes. I'll call you otherwise."

He got out of bed and crossed the room to her, then bent and placed a soft kiss on her lips. "Last night was unbelievable."

"Yeah," she said, smiling.

Frustrating as hell, but unbelievable.

She turned and left the room. Outside in the hallway,

she tapped on her door and waited for Lauren to answer. A few moments later, the door swung open, and her friend peered at her from behind a mop of dark hair hanging in front of her face.

"What do you do at night—pretend you're at a heavy metal concert?"

"I just finished drying my hair, smart ass."

"You want to get breakfast at the buffet?" Macy asked, only to find herself being grabbed and pulled into the room without ceremony.

Lauren closed the door and started brushing her long mop of hair into submission. "Of course I do, but don't start acting all casual like you have nothing to tell me about last night."

"I don't really have anything to tell you."

"It's my theory you're proving here. I deserve details."

"You want the truth? Okay, your idea about manipulating results in my favor sucks the big one. It doesn't take into account guys like Griffin, who are so determined to make a girl come that they're willing to stay up all night to make it happen."

"You screwed all night?"

"No, I finally wore him out for good around two in the morning."

"Bet you deserve another award for faking it," Lauren said, not even trying to hide her amusement. "Maybe even a trophy case full of them."

"Yeah, that would be great to show guests at my apartment."

"I told you, you've just got to learn to enjoy the endorphins."

"I enjoyed the hell out of those endorphins, but I still wanted more."

Lauren went into the bathroom where she could look in the mirror as she put the final touches on her hairdo.

"Seriously," Macy said, following her. "This is way harder than I thought it would be. Griffin thinks he's a sex superhero or something. It was crazy the lengths he went to—even after I did my best acting."

She sat down on the edge of the huge hot tub that dominated the bathroom.

"He didn't even buy my first acting attempt—well, not completely."

Lauren looked at her wide-eyed through the mirror "He figured out you were faking it?"

"He asked, but I managed to convince him he was wrong. I thought I'd done a pretty convincing job."

"You're an award-winning orgasm actress. I'm sure you gave a great performance."

"Ha-ha. After that first time, he kicked it into high gear and made sure he tried extra hard to make me come for the rest of the night."

"Sounds like…fun."

"I just don't get how he could have figured me out."

"Some guys actually pay attention to the signs," Lauren said so casually that if Macy hadn't been a witness, she never would have guessed this whole faking-it thing had been her idea in the first place.

"That's wonderful. So I've probably lucked into the one guy in a million who can read a woman's body."

"Hey…" Lauren shrugged. "If it weren't for bad luck, you'd have no luck at all."

"You're just overflowing with crap today, aren't you?"

Lauren suppressed a smile. "I'm sensing hostility. Not an uncommon side effect of sexual deprivation."

"Is my whole life just one big science experiment to you?"

"Basically," Lauren said, and had Macy not known her better she might have believed her. "What I'm really interested in hearing more about, though, is the actual experience. Did you notice him having any immediate dumbed-down effects?"

"I thought you already had your results. Spare me the microscope."

Lauren stared at her, the stubborn set of her mouth making it clear she wanted an answer.

"I didn't come. He did. End of story. If you want to know the results, you can just wait and see what happens on Monday."

Lauren's expression changed from annoyed to amused, and she launched into a bad Jimmy Buffet version of "Come Monday."

"Thank you for ruining that song for me."

"Takes on a whole new meaning, doesn't it?"

"I suppose it would if I had any intention of sleeping with Griffin again after this weekend is done."

Lauren went into the bathroom and began fixing her hair in the mirror. "Why wouldn't you? I mean, if you need a little relief from all the action you're getting now…"

Good question. Why wouldn't she? Well, there was the obvious. "Because I'm going to be his boss soon? Isn't that a good enough reason?"

"I guess if you're going to be all anal-retentive about it, sure."

"Oh, shut up."

"Seriously, though, you're right. Once you've been promoted, no screwing around with the office help is a good rule to follow. But until then, why can't you get yours?"

Macy sighed and went out into the main room to find an outfit. Bright sunlight poured through the wall of windows that overlooked the balcony and outside. Even though it was only ten in the morning, the sounds pouring in from a door Lauren had left open were of a city wide awake.

Macy went to the open door, inhaled the hot desert air and then closed it. "How can you stand all that heat pouring in here?"

Lauren came out of the bathroom with her long dark hair smoothed into a shiny curtain and shrugged. "I thought it felt kind of nice. I like the dry air."

"I already took a shower, but I still need to change clothes and then we can go. Griffin and Carson are probably already waiting downstairs for us."

"You didn't answer my question—why can't you get it on with Griffin until the promotion happens?"

"Maybe I don't want to." Macy avoided eye contact as she went to the closet and rummaged around for the appropriate outfit.

Lauren's knowing gaze seemed to be burning a hole into her back. "That's not true. You're into him."

"I am not," Macy said, trying her best to sound

casual, when actually, the accusation struck her as, at best, infuriating.

How could she, a self-respecting woman with excellent taste in men, be into a guy who clearly thought so much of himself? She couldn't.

More likely, she was just into the whole idea of a weekend fling with her adolescent-fantasy guy. And maybe the sexual frustration thing was clouding her otherwise good judgment.

She selected a beaded green camisole and a matching purple-and-green skirt to wear, then went into the bathroom to change. Once dressed, she found a pair of platform espadrilles to complete the outfit, and when she turned to Lauren, her friend gave her another one of those all-knowing looks.

"Don't kid yourself—you're into him."

Macy rolled her eyes and threw up her hands in defeat. "Believe what you want. And what exactly is your story again? You're a freewheeling flight attendant from Atlanta?"

"San Francisco."

They walked to the elevator, rode it to the casino level and walked to the buffet. The Golden Gate Casino's breakfast layout turned out to be an impressive one, complete with seafood and dessert and just about everything else Macy could think of.

They spotted Griffin and Carson across the room and gave them a little wave, then went to load up their plates.

"Okay, he looks doable," Lauren said as she selected several gigantic strawberries.

"Told you."

"And you're sure he's not obnoxious? I can't tolerate obnoxiousness."

"He's fun. Really fun. I promise."

"So why haven't you dated him?"

Macy piled a couple of huge wedges of French toast onto her plate. "I don't know. I guess he's never shown any particular interest. Maybe he's not into blondes."

"Every guy is into blondes who look like you."

She made a face at Lauren. "Whatever."

"I bet I know. Griffin is into you—probably has been for years—and Carson knows it. He doesn't want to step on his friend's toes."

"That's ridiculous. Griffin and I have never gotten along in the office."

"Sexual tension can do that."

They moved farther down the buffet, and Macy found herself torn between fruit crepes and eggs Benedict. She was running out of room on her plate.

"I don't know why you think you can take a tiny bit of information and extrapolate entire relationship histories based on almost nothing."

Lauren's mysterious little smile would have been more infuriating if Macy hadn't been so used to it. And Lauren's extrapolations themselves would have been more infuriating if she wasn't so often correct.

"There's no other explanation. If Carson has never flirted with you, it's because he knows his friend wants you."

"I'm so glad you know everything. It must make life a breeze for you."

"Yeah, and I'm pretty handy to have around, aren't I?"

Lauren had an uncanny way of ignoring sarcasm when she wanted to, and piling it on thick when it helped her make a point.

They carried their plates to the table where Carson and Griffin were sitting with cups of coffee, and Macy went through the usual introductions.

The guys went off to grab their own plates of food, and as soon as they were gone, Lauren pinned Macy with a look that said she approved of Carson.

"He's hot," she said. "Very hot."

"Told you. Too bad you're just a flight attendant looking for a weekend fling, because I think you and Carson could hit it off."

Lauren stabbed a strawberry, her expression blasé. "I'm holding out for a wealthy foreign national so I can snag dual citizenship for someplace cool like Monaco."

"Right, because we bump into so many wealthy foreign nationals in our everyday lives. That makes perfect sense."

"In my flight-attendant career, I meet them all the time. And I think a girl has to stick to her guns, keep her standards high and all that." Her attention was on the gigantic strawberry now.

"You're just afraid of finding a guy you could really fall for and then having to face the big C-word."

"Cunnilingus? I'm all for it."

Macy tried to keep a straight face but failed. "*Commitment,* smart ass."

Lauren made a face and shuddered. "You're right about that. I'm so *not* the marriage-and-kids type. I might as well get it tattooed on my forehead, so the guys who are can just avoid the disappointment."

"Or you can keep using false identities and pretending to be a footloose flight attendant. What's your fake name, by the way?"

"I could do without the acidic disapproval. And my name's Lauren Smith."

"That's creative."

"It's easy to remember, okay, *smart ass?*"

Macy spotted the guys headed in their direction, and she lowered her voice. "Okay, Lauren Smith. Just be sure not to let him see your driver's license, and when you're lamenting the fact that you've lost a perfectly good guy, don't cry to me about it."

But she knew her words were falling on indifferent ears. Lauren had never, and probably would never, find one guy she could settle for. Macy almost admired her insatiable appetite for variety, but unlike Lauren, she believed that there was even more satisfaction to be had in finding one guy with whom she could develop a soul-deep connection.

When she glanced up at Griffin sitting down at their table again, he flashed a knowing little smile that spoke volumes about what was on his mind, and she knew without a doubt that he was not one of those guys. Theirs was a surface connection, born purely of sexual hormones, misguided adolescent dreams and frustration.

"Either of you have anything in mind you'd like to see today?" Griffin asked.

"I'm open to whatever," Macy said. "I guess we

should check out everything here at the hotel before we venture out."

"So far I'm pretty impressed," Carson said. "I've stayed at a lot of Vegas hotels, but this one actually manages to look more classy than cheesy."

"Isn't it kind of cheesy to use the word *classy?*" Griffin said, his green eyes sparking with mischief.

"Shut up," Carson said. "You know what I mean."

"It's true," Lauren said. "This is the first Vegas hotel I've seen that manages to do over-the-top in a really tasteful way."

Macy ate her French toast as she listened to them talking about possible marketing strategies. Lauren, intelligent as she was, had plenty to offer despite the fact that it wasn't her industry. Macy had her own thoughts about the slant to take on the campaign, but they were still simmering in her head, and she didn't like to share her ideas while they were still half-baked.

In fact, her creative process was probably part of what had always sparked tension between herself and Griffin. It drove him crazy when she held back during brainstorming sessions.

And while she could see that maybe she came off as not a team player, she believed that some of the best inspirations only became diluted when worked on by committee. She preferred to develop her thoughts until they were fully formed and could have the most impact. Then, and only then, would she present them and make herself open to feedback.

By the time she'd finished most of her breakfast, the conversation had turned from ad campaigns to Vegas attractions to Lauren's faux career as a flight attendant. The guys were listening attentively as she spun lie after lie about herself, and Macy marveled at the ease with which she did it.

"So you've probably traveled all over the world then," Carson said.

Lauren nodded. That part, at least, was true. Lauren's family had money—lots and lots of money— and they never hesitated to send their daughter on exotic trips, with or without them.

"What's your favorite place you've ever visited?" Carson asked.

While Macy had thought Lauren's answer would be Paris, she surprised her. "Romania, believe it or not."

"Really? What was it that you liked?"

"The whole Carpathian mountain region, with all its dark legends about Dracula—it really got to me. Something about it resonated, and I could see why those legends developed. It's really a haunting, mysterious place. Not like anywhere else I've ever been."

"Wow."

"Are you one of those goth chicks who's all into vampires and stuff?" Carson asked, sounding vaguely turned on by the idea.

Macy tried not to laugh. "Maybe she's a little designer goth."

Lauren narrowed her eyes at Macy. "Am I now?"

"You're always wearing dark colors, and you've got the dark hair and pale skin…."

"First, this is my natural coloring, and second, we

live in San Francisco. You just described ninety percent of the population."

"And you've got that funky altar in your house."

"It's not an altar. It's just some damn candles. On a shelf." Lauren's voice had turned a little stiff, and her expression had lost its usual cool detachment. Now her mouth was set in a grim, sarcastic line.

Macy had never seen her get flustered like this before. As though she was trying not to, but it wasn't working. Maybe she just didn't want to be teased in front of a guy she wanted to score with.

"Hey, I think if we sit here much longer I might be tempted to eat more food. Why don't we skip out of here and go find some trouble to get into," Carson said, his timing impeccable.

"Yeah, this being Macy's first time in Vegas, she's got lots of trouble to find."

Carson glanced at his watch. "I was thinking of doing a little gambling. Anyone interested?"

Lauren's grim expression vanished. "That sounds right up my alley."

"I don't know." Macy glanced at Griffin. "Do you want to split up, maybe catch up again at dinner time?"

The last thing she needed was Carson around taking notes on every little thing that happened between her and Griffin, and she didn't really feel like gambling right after breakfast, anyway. She figured she'd played the odds enough last night with her ten minutes on the slots.

"I'm cool with that." Griffin looked at Carson. "We were thinking of catching the show at the Golden Gate last night, but we got, um, sidetracked. Want us to pick up tickets for all of us for a show tonight?"

Carson shrugged and looked at Lauren. "You game?"

"Absolutely."

"We're there. What do you say we meet up for dinner around seven?"

They decided to make reservations at one of the hotel restaurants, then catch up via cell phone to confirm the final plans. Five minutes later, the two couples had parted ways, and Macy and Griffin headed out into the blinding desert sunlight through a huge rotating brass door.

After the dark, artificial world of the hotel, the outdoors seemed unreal. And truly not much about Vegas seemed real, not the Technicolor blue of the sky, not the spectacle of the architecture, not the constant bustle of the crowds.

The unreal atmosphere renewed Macy's sense that she could break all the rules this weekend. That here in the desert, she could do everything wrong, and she'd still be all right. She could take risks, sleep with the wrong man, tell lies for fun and profit.

In a city where nothing was as it seemed, Macy felt as if she fit right in.

Macy Thomaston, Queen of the Fake Orgasm, performing tonight at the Golden Gate Resort and Casino, Las Vegas. This weekend only.

8

GRIFFIN YAWNED and stretched out on the hotel balcony's chaise longue. He hadn't intended to doze off, but Macy was wearing him out. In a good way.

They'd wandered the strip for a little while after breakfast, until it got so hot they couldn't stand it anymore. Then they'd explored every inch of the Golden Gate, trying to absorb the feel of it, all of its sights and sounds that might influence the ad campaign. But that had inevitably led them to decide that the private suites were the nicest feature in the hotel and they really needed to spend more time in one of them. For the sake of research, of course.

An afternoon of sex with Macy was by far the best product research Griffin had ever done.

Next to him sat the cart from room service they'd ordered for a late lunch and hadn't bothered to move back into the hallway yet. And overhead, the pink-and-orange-streaked sky in the waning light suggested it was getting close to dinnertime.

From inside the room, he could hear Macy talking on the phone, something about meeting up with them for dinner and that they had tickets for an eight o'clock show. Probably talking to Lauren.

He couldn't remember the last time he'd had so much sex in so short a time. Hell, he could hardly remember his name right now. Griffin Something-or-Other. Did he even have a middle name? It started with an M. Mitchell? No, Michael. That was it. Griffin Michael Reed.

Whew. Good. He hadn't completely lost it.

Macy appeared on the balcony again, wearing his white button-down shirt, open in the front, and nothing else. He smiled at the sight, even as his body responded in its predictable fashion.

"You might as well not have bothered getting dressed," he said, only then noticing that he was still naked.

She looked down at herself. "Oh, I just put this on to move the cart back into the hallway, but I remembered I needed to call Lauren, and then I forgot about the cart, and—"

He grabbed her arm and pulled her down on top of him, where she fit quite nicely. He slid his hands over her bare ass, savoring her full curves, letting his fingertips tickle the cleft of her backside as his cock strained against her belly.

"Do we have time for one more round before dinner?"

Macy grinned. "You're insatiable."

"Only for you, baby."

"I bet you say that to all your future bosses." She started kissing his neck so he took that as a yes and shifted her hips until she was within target range.

"If it turns you on to think that…" he said, teasing.

He didn't want to get into an argument about the imminent promotion now, not when he had much more important matters to attend to.

He reached for a condom from the half-empty box on the side table next to them, and a minute later he was suited up and ready for liftoff.

"I told Lauren I'd meet her in my room in fifteen minutes."

"So we'll go fast."

She shifted her hips, and he eased into her. She must have been a little sore from all their lovemaking, but if so, she didn't complain.

Something about her expression when she sat up and looked at him gave Griffin pause, though. "Is something wrong?"

"I just realized tomorrow's Sunday, and we'll be flying back to the real world."

With his cock buried all the way inside her, he didn't feel much equipped to carry on a conversation, but he was willing to give it a shot.

"So we live it up tonight."

But he didn't want it to end, either. He'd only seen Macy as a sex object at work, as someone to lust after and compete with. Now that he was getting to know her, he liked her. A lot. Maybe too much.

Without realizing it, he'd been hoping he wouldn't like her so that they could have this affair and then get back to business on Monday. Liking her complicated things.

"Yeah," she said, the tension easing from her expression. "We live it up tonight. I like that."

Her breasts peeking out of his shirt was a sight

almost too sweet for words. "You're beautiful," he said, anyway.

She rode him a little faster now, her tightness and heat nearly all his mind could focus on. But still, there were these other thoughts vying for his attention.

Thoughts about Macy. About having her for more than just tonight.

Her shallow breathing told him she was close to coming, and he slipped his fingers between their bodies, coaxing her closer to orgasm. When her muscles started contracting around him, and she cried out in throaty gasps, he joined her.

Her body convulsed as he spilled into her, and the pleasure that rocked his body was like a drug he couldn't get enough of. He was addicted to Macy, and he was in serious trouble.

He wrapped his arms around her and pulled her close, then placed a kiss on her damp forehead as they caught their breath again.

"Wow," she said. "I didn't think I could do that again so soon."

"Me, either. Do you think this is some kind of medical problem—our inability to stop having sex?"

She laughed. "If it is, I don't want to have to explain it to a doctor."

"I'm thinking we could be in big trouble at work on Monday."

"No, we'll just have to make sure we, um, do everything we can tonight."

"You think that will help?"

She shrugged, standing up from the chair, and

another melancholy expression crossed her face. "I'd better go get dressed for dinner. We'll knock when we're ready, okay?"

Griffin nodded, then watched as she walked away.

He could hear her changing clothes inside the room, but he didn't have the heart to face her again, because all of a sudden he was wondering why she looked so sad, and he wasn't sure he wanted to know the truth.

WHILE MACY got herself ready for dinner, Lauren filled her in on the day she'd spent with Carson, gambling and then…not gambling. They'd apparently taken to each other pretty quickly and had spent the afternoon in Carson's suite.

"I don't really need any more details," Macy called from the dresser when she sensed that Lauren was about to launch into a full-on description of Carson's more impressive attributes. "I have to work with the man."

"That certainly didn't stop you from getting down and dirty with Griffin."

Macy decided not to point out all the things that were wrong with Lauren reminding her of that. Instead, she stared at her hair in the mirror, trying to decide if she should wear it up or down.

"You can't possibly be planning to wear that in public?" Macy said when Lauren emerged from the bathroom wearing a black dress so tiny if she'd blinked she would have missed it.

"You think it's too much?" Lauren asked, checking herself out in the mirror, turning this way and that.

"I think it's too little. I mean, really, I feel like I'm getting way too much personal info."

"But this is Vegas. We're supposed to dress like trashy girls here."

"Only if we want to be mistaken for hookers."

Lauren rolled her eyes. "I forgot to pack my church dress. Do you have any other recommendations?"

Macy went to the closet and checked out the assortment of outfits Lauren had brought. Lots of club attire. Nothing that left any details to the imagination. "What about this orange dress?"

"Won't it make me look like I'm trying too hard?"

"You're wearing *that,* and you're worried about looking like you're trying too hard? Aren't you maybe a little worried that you'll look like you want it too badly?"

"I do want it badly."

"You just don't want to look like you have to work to get it."

"Exactly."

Macy shook her head at Lauren's warped logic. "That makes perfect sense."

"I can do without the sarcasm."

"Wear what you want. I'm officially done with the subject."

Lauren stepped into a pair of black stiletto heels that made her legs look several feet longer. She was already tall and on the slim side, though she had the sort of stacked hips and chest that made guys stop in their tracks and stare. The dress and heels made it all too much. Too sexy, if there was such a thing.

She'd curled her long dark hair, and it hung in slight waves that would probably be gone after a night of hard dancing. Her dark red lipstick—Lauren's signature—contrasted with her dark hair and fair skin, making her face so striking it was impossible not to look at her.

"So are you ready to deliver Griffin's IQ its death blow tonight?"

Macy winced at the reminder of another night of sex that would end without satisfaction for at least one of them. She'd discovered a whole new facet to the problem of faking it today. All this selfless pleasure was making her like Griffin a little too much. It was impossible not to like a guy she'd spent so much time pleasuring, and who had exerted such an extraordinary amount of energy trying to pleasure her right back.

"I guess I'm as ready as I'll ever be."

"Remember," Lauren said, "the wilder the sex, the more dramatic the results."

"How, exactly, did you measure that scientifically?"

Lauren smiled. "Various methods. We used surveys that were filled out after sexual encounters, and we also used a lot of horny college students getting off under more controlled conditions.

"They agreed to masturbate, with varying degrees of stimulation. Some of them got something really lame like a typical mail-order catalog to masturbate to, and some got mildly stimulating images, while some got really hot porn—or erotica, depending on personal preferences.

"After each test subject achieved orgasm, they had

to do various cognitive tests. Invariably, the hotter the stimulus or encounter, the more dramatic the results."

"That's just…bizarre."

Lauren shrugged. "It's science."

"No wonder you wouldn't talk about any details of your study for the past few years. What could you have said—I'm measuring the results of masturbation in horny college students?"

"I didn't talk about it because I didn't want anyone else homing in on my field of study."

"I wouldn't have, I can guarantee you that."

"No, but you might have accidentally told someone else."

"Are you ever going to trust me completely?"

Lauren looked doubtful. "Sorry. Being secretive is just an old habit I can't break, I guess."

And it was true. Lauren was one of those people who never revealed much about herself, even to her closest friends. It made it hard to get close to her, but Macy had known her since freshman year in college and had always felt a connection to her that she couldn't explain. It was as if they'd been friends in a past life—as if many things between them could just remain unspoken, and it would be okay. They understood each other.

But it still bothered Macy sometimes that she had to nag and prod her best friend to talk about the simplest details of her life.

She turned her thoughts back to her more immediate dilemma. "So, the wilder the sex, the harder the IQ falls…that could be the title of your study."

Lauren laughed. "Maybe—*The Wilder They Are*—I like it. If I were publishing it in *Cosmo*. The medical journals usually run a little more conservative, sadly."

Macy glanced at the clock on the nightstand. They had ten minutes before they were supposed to meet the guys in the lobby.

"You're really wearing that dress, aren't you?" Macy said, looking down at herself. She was wearing a much more conservative Marilyn Monroe-inspired frock that made her look as though she was on her way to a country jamboree when she stood next to Lauren.

"Why don't you wear my orange dress?"

"You think it will fit?" Macy did love the orange dress. It had a disco fever vibe that appealed to her.

"I'm sure it will. It'll be longer on you than it is on me, but it's stretchy."

Macy changed into the much skimpier dress, borrowed Lauren's silver heels, and in five minutes they were out the door, ready for trouble.

But no matter how ready she might have looked, Macy had a growing sense of foreboding, as if she was getting herself into a much bigger mess with Griffin that she'd ever anticipated.

Yet, the damage was done, and some kinds of trouble were too good to back out of.

MACY HAD CONSUMED perhaps a wee bit too much wine during the show they'd caught after dinner, and now she was buzzing nicely as she sat in a comfortable leather sofa next to Griffin at the jazz lounge they'd all wandered into afterward. The lights were low, the music was subdued and the tables and chairs were set up to invite conversation. It was the ideal kind of place to chat with friends.

In fact, she found herself wishing this wasn't just a one-time occurrence. As a group, they worked nicely. At least in Las Vegas they did. Maybe in the real world they'd all grate on each other's nerves to no end.

"Do we dare talk shop again on vacation time?" Griffin asked, looking around the table at everyone.

Carson shrugged. "Technically, this isn't vacation, since we're here on the resort's dime."

"Don't mind me," Lauren said. "I've been around Macy long enough to know how she thinks—always looking for the angle that sells."

Griffin's eyebrows quirked upward. "Is that right?"

Macy sank into her seat a bit. It sounded so sleazy when they put it like that. But it was true. She loved figuring out what any given thing's appeal was, and then emphasizing it.

She smiled. "I'm an ad girl, what can I say?"

"So let's say Carson is our product? How do we sell him?" Griffin asked.

Carson made an attempt at looking offended. "I'm not for sale."

"Hypothetical, man," Griffin said, keeping his attention on Macy.

"That's easy," she said. "Charm, good looks, great sense of humor. Carson's an easy sell. Advertising could be totally stylized, evoking a mood of sexy coolness rather than trying to point out any obvious product attributes."

Carson beamed. "I knew there was a reason I liked you so much, Macy."

Lauren looked unconvinced. "I don't like those ads that don't even say the name of the product."

Macy nodded. "They're a risky move, and really only for companies whose brands are already highly recognizable. They're more about keeping products in the public consciousness, making sure a household name brand is associated with a hip image than they are about directly selling."

"But it's all about selling in the end," Griffin added, then polished off the last of his martini.

"Maybe we've just stumbled onto the future of dating," Lauren said. "People's lives keep getting busier, there's less time for dating around, less time for meeting new people. Maybe there could be a channel on TV you tune into just to see people commercials."

"Or it could be on the Internet—an extension of dating services. Everyone has a commercial, except they're the product," Macy added.

"I think those already exist," Griffin said. "Not that I've done the Internet dating thing. But I've heard of some sites having videos."

"Okay, maybe I'm not as innovative as I thought." Macy smiled in a self-deprecating way. "Or maybe the commercials will get more sophisticated over time."

Lauren grinned. "More and more sophisticated, until Carson's not even in his own commercial. You just see a stylish apartment, empty, to signify his need for a girlfriend, some hip music playing, and maybe a photo of him on a bookshelf. The camera pans across the room, not even pausing on the photo. It stops at the table, where two glasses of wine sit next to two elegant table settings. And then the word *Imagine* flashes on the screen. Then, fade to black. No number to call. Maybe just a Web site to log on to."

Everyone laughed.

Griffin said, "Lauren, I think you've missed your calling. You should work in advertising."

She rolled her eyes. "Sorry, but I think you're all pimps. Product pimps."

He smiled. "I can live with that."

"I've been called worse," Carson said. "Besides, Lauren seems pretty happy with the flight-attendant life. It's rare I meet someone who actually likes what they do for a living."

Macy cast Lauren a pregnant glance. What would have been the harm in telling the truth about her job? Well, okay, so maybe Macy didn't know what it was like to have a career that turned guys off. She was better off just minding her own business, she reminded herself. Better off keeping her mouth shut.

Lauren was a smart girl. She knew what she was doing.

"So what about our real ad campaign? We ought to be focusing our thoughts by now, coming up with some preliminary ideas."

Macy settled farther into the plush sofa, pleasantly conscious of Griffin's nearness. When she recrossed her legs and he casually placed a hand on her thigh, her insides started buzzing. She wanted him more with each passing hour, wanted to toss aside a few IQ points and indulge in whatever came, but…she couldn't give up now. She'd set the plan into motion, and backing out halfway through would be stupid at best.

"The campaign will be both print and television, right?" Carson asked.

"And we'll be overseeing the Web site redesign to match the campaign," Griffin said.

"I'm thinking of something that captures the feel of the gold coast in its first heyday. Wealth from the gold rush that brought San Francisco into its own. Glamour, a touch of the roaring twenties…"

"How do we tie that into Las Vegas and its current appeal as a place of debauchery?" Macy asked.

Griffin said, "We've got these disparate elements— the hotel's elegance, the high-roller culture, the whole Las Vegas scene and then the nod to all things San Francisco. It's a lot to mesh."

Macy's brain worked its way around the problem. She had a few ideas, and she'd been mulling them over long enough that she felt as if they were ready to be presented to the group.

"Let's see…all the casinos have certain things in common, and people already know what goes on in Vegas, so we have to capture what's unique about this resort, while also reminding the audience of why they'll want to come here."

"So maybe we feature a beautiful, scantily-clad woman, a young successful-looking guy and the elegant backdrop of the resort," Carson said.

"It's been done." Macy said. "A lot."

"Maybe we do a montage of images, or…" Griffin

was just thinking out loud, so Macy refrained from pointing out that a montage of images was about as obvious and uncreative as they could get.

And then she realized, maybe the sex was working. Maybe he really was dumbed down enough for it to be noticeable. She tried not to smile. "Okay, so if the enviable guy and girl have been done, maybe we do a variation on it. We take the obvious and spin it in a unique way."

"Maybe it's a guy and a guy, or a girl and a girl—it is the Golden Gate resort, after all…"

"Girl and girl, I'm all for," Carson said, then dodged Lauren's elbow. She cast a sideways glare at him, but Macy knew she wasn't offended. Lauren was about as accepting of people's sexual proclivities as a girl could get.

"I'm thinking we'll miss a big chunk of our target audience if we did that. I've got these images in my head of the Golden Gate Bridge, a view of San Francisco from the water and maybe a fade into… No, wait, here's an idea— There's an image of the front door of the hotel, and inside the door is the view of the bridge and the city."

Silent nodding from Griffin and Carson. Lauren was busy trying to hail a waitress for another drink.

"It's interesting," Griffin finally said. "But aside from maybe luxury and a sense of escape, what does it really convey that we're looking for?"

Macy shrugged. "Nothing." Years of creativity by committee had taught her not to take criticism personally and never to fall in love with her own ideas.

"If we want to convey the idea that this resort is a

cut above the standard Vegas fare, maybe we need to go totally different in the advertising—do something no one else is doing," Griffin said.

"Have you studied the competition's advertising?" Carson asked.

"I spent a few nights on the Internet checking out everything I could," Griffin said.

Macy nodded. "Me, too."

"Oh, right. I forgot you two are in a race for the big promotion, trying to out-creative each other."

Macy shifted in her seat, definitely not keen on the new direction of the conversation. Then a flash of brilliance hit.

"I've got it," she said. "What about something minimalist, something understated, to send the message that this resort is so nice, no manipulative images are needed."

Carson smiled. "Which in itself is a manipulative image. I like it."

"It's been done before, of course. Lots of upscale brands are going minimalist," Griffin said, always the one to find the weak spot.

"True," Macy said. "But what about…say, opulent minimalist. Magazine ad—picture a blank metallic gold page, some kind of elegant font, and something like 'Welcome to Luxury,' printed center page."

"I like it," Griffin said.

"And maybe the page could open up. Either split down the middle like doors, or a fold-out page, with more about the resort inside," Carson said.

Macy nodded. "Maybe. Or the call to action could

be on the opposite page. Still an all-gold page. But the centered text on that page could just be the name of the resort, the location, Web site and phone number."

"That definitely sounds like a possible direction for the print campaign," Carson said. "Keep thinking about it. It just gave me an idea for the television ads. Same minimalist aesthetic. Maybe a black screen, some really sexy jazz music and the same words flashing on screen."

"I think there needs to be some kind of visual besides the words. What if we have images of the hotel itself flashing on screen…but," Macy paused, ideas competing for attention in her brain. "I just feel like this is a chance for us to do something really edgy and sexy for television. There aren't many casinos doing TV ads, so we're not in such a saturated format."

"Maybe this is where the hot guy and girl could work," Carson said.

Macy nodded. "That's what I'm thinking. Maybe the camera follows them, it's late at night, they're wandering the casino, the hotel, maybe making out in the elevator, and then it ends when they enter their hotel room and close the door."

"You don't think that's too risqué?" Griffin asked. "I mean, considering the hotel's overall image?"

"It's all in how it's handled," Carson said. "And where the ads run. We could go from PG-rated to R-rated depending on the audience."

All this work talk was reminding Macy of her relationship with Griffin and its true nature. They'd been competitors, not lovers, before yesterday. And she could tell just by the tone of his voice that when it came to business, he wasn't about personal connections.

He was all about business.

It wouldn't matter to him what happened between them in bed, so it shouldn't matter to her, either. And it didn't, so long as he showed up at work forgetful and foggy-brained.

"I like that," Lauren said. "I think that kind of ad would catch my interest."

"Maybe if we continue the 'Welcome to…' theme, then this ad could fade to black and the words *Welcome to Debauchery* or something like that could flash on-screen."

Griffin's eyes lit up. "Now you're talking. It sounds a little like the Absolut vodka ads. In fact, we could do something similar, in that the 'Welcome to…' message could change depending on the target audience."

"The ads could follow this couple around having different experiences for each message. There could be 'Welcome to Luxury,' 'Welcome to Decadence,' 'Welcome to Relaxation.'" Even as she continued the brainstorming, Macy's hopes sank a little. Griffin's contribution was the first good idea he'd come up with since their discussion had begun. She'd been imagining him as a slack-jawed yokel come Monday morning, but that was probably wishing for too much.

In fact, any kind of hope at all may have been too much when it was based on such a crazy plan as hers. Had she lost her mind? Maybe she was the one who'd been screwed too many times.

Macy bit her lip and wondered if she was tossing

aside her professionalism for no good reason at all. But then one glance at Griffin, one surge of attraction that shot from her heart right to her groin, and she knew. Even if she was screwed, it wouldn't be that bad so long as it was with Griffin.

9

MACY AND CARSON continued to discuss the campaign, debating innovative executional techniques and tossing out word and image pairings, searching for that elusive cutting edge the client wanted.

"I think we've got a good start here," Griffin finally interrupted after adding little else to the conversation. "Let's keep it all on the table, but for now, we'd better stop before we bore Lauren to death."

Lauren looked up from her cosmopolitan; she'd been trying to catch the cherry floating in it. Macy hadn't even noticed the waitress bringing her another one.

"Don't mind me," Lauren said. "I'm just here for the alcohol."

"And the company, right?" Carson said, trying on his best forlorn-puppy-dog expression.

"Oh, right, and the company."

"Anyone up for dancing?" Carson asked.

"I guess we should try out the discotheque, too—it's part of the whole resort experience." Except Macy usually required another drink or two before she was fully able to enjoy herself on the dance floor without worrying that she looked like a rhythm-challenged white girl.

"It's eleven—the club is probably hopping by now," Lauren said as she glanced at the tiny black watch on her wrist.

Griffin laid some cash on the table to cover the tip for the waitress, and they left the bar, making their way across the casino and up one level to the nightclub. It wasn't hard to find it. One needed only to follow the sound of thumping bass, the din of people talking over loud music and the trail of scantily clad women and eager-looking guys headed in that direction.

Macy loved people-watching, but especially so here in Vegas, where the entire country—and to a lesser extent the entire world—converged to indulge in their basest desires. The lure of easy money, easy sex and free-flowing liquor brought people to this place like nowhere else. Grandmas in sweat suits; midwesterners in white sneakers, jeans and T-shirts; college girls wearing clothes they clearly never wore in real life and acting in ways they probably never did in real life, either, tourists from Europe and Asia...

Not even San Francisco had that draw on people. It lost out when it came to the luridness factor. Which was part of the reason the big casinos stole their charm from other locations. They may not have had the beauty of Venice, but with enough money, they could build a replica of the city, minus the pigeons.

And they might not have had the cosmopolitan flair of San Francisco, but no doubt, money could build a good semblance of the city's allure.

There was no line at the door of the nightclub, so they paid the cover charge, then entered the world of darkness and flashing lights and pulsating bodies. The club was called Sensation, and the music seemed to be a European-influenced house sound. At the moment, anyway.

They wandered around until they found a small opening on the dance floor, and Lauren and Carson went their own way.

Macy leaned over to say into Griffin's ear, "Do you like to dance?"

He smiled. "It's a little late to be asking me that, don't you think?"

But his body answered for him. He started moving to the music as though he'd been born on a dance floor, and Macy was immediately…impressed. She should have known such an all-around athlete would know what to do with his body no matter what the situation.

She'd always liked dancing, but she did enough of it alone in front of her bedroom mirror to feel a little weird dancing in front of an audience. She'd never been big on the club scene, but that was more because of her introverted nature than anything else. In truth, she loved going out clubbing once a few drinks got her past the awkward self-consciousness of dancing with a crowd of other people.

Griffin's hands were on her hips now, and she watched him as they moved in time, their hips drifting closer and closer until they were pressed together, their legs intertwined, their bodies pulsing to the music. She followed his lead, and when their gazes locked, there was no more worry about how she looked or if she had enough rhythm.

She just danced.

After a while, she realized she was doing pretty damn well, which gave her even more confidence to just get her groove on and forget everything else. Griffin made it all so easy.

Their brainstorming session had given her a wakeup call, had reminded her of why she was here and what the goal was. There was no room for turning into a soft-hearted girly girl now, not this late in the game.

And having Griffin's hard, capable body against hers reminded her that as far as games went, she was playing a pretty damn fun one.

Macy wasn't sure how much time had passed or how many songs they'd danced through by the time she realized they were both drenched in sweat. Her feet ached in Lauren's high heels, and her hair clung to her face in damp tendrils. Probably all her makeup was gone by now, and she imagined she could use a nice dip in the suite's hot tub.

Which was one of the few hotel features she hadn't tried out with Griffin yet.

When she took his hand and led him off the dance floor, he didn't resist. He had no idea she was leading him straight to his own intellectual doom. And thanks to their having stepped back into work mode for that short while tonight, she wasn't even feeling guilty about it.

Well, maybe the alcohol had something to do with

her lack of guilt. She could only hope she wasn't so tipsy that she'd accidentally screw away a few of her own IQ points as well.

GRIFFIN LEANED IN through the bathroom doorway and watched, his mouth dry and his cock hardening by the second, as Macy stripped off her dress, shimmied out of her panties and stepped into the bubbling hot tub.

Damn it, she was hot. He wouldn't have been surprised if the water had started bubbling only after she'd entered it.

He admired the long lines of her legs, the delicious fullness of her ass, the curve of her waist and the satin expanse of her back. Her wavy blond hair brushed her shoulders, and he ached to see it all wet, damp ringlets of it clinging to her face as they made love the way it had when they'd been sweaty and dancing.

She turned and smiled. "Are you going to join me or just watch?"

"Watching is pretty damn fun."

One corner of her mouth curved up, and she sank into the water, sitting down. The water rose to her underarms, enveloping all that delicious flesh he wanted to see, to touch, to possess.

Macy leaned back, closing her eyes, then she bent all the way back and dipped her head under. When she emerged, her hair was slicked against her head and her face glistened with rivulets of water trickling down.

Griffin ached to join her, and yet he couldn't move

from his position at the door. He was riveted by the sight of her.

"You can't just stand there watching. I'm useless as a performer."

"Far from it. You don't even have to perform. You're just amazing to look at."

She smiled. "Treasured words for a girl who was the class dork."

"I don't believe you about that, you know."

"Believe it. I went through a major chubby phase during middle and high school, I had no sense of style and I always got the wrong haircut."

"I'm sure you were gorgeous."

"I had braces, too—for six years. And glasses. Way too much facial hardware."

"You wear contacts now?"

She nodded. "Guys used to call me the Float. As in, they were implying I was so big I looked like a Macy's Thanksgiving Day Parade float. Clever, huh?"

"They were all assholes."

"True, and I certainly wasn't as big as a parade float, but I couldn't get a boyfriend. I didn't lose my virginity until college."

"Intentionally?"

"No! I couldn't give it away. I mean, the most attention I ever got from the guys at my high school was when I'd walk down the hallway and they'd yell, 'Look out, it's the Float' and all plaster themselves against the walls like a Mack truck was coming through."

"Total assholes. But as far as the virginity thing, you

were lucky. I have distinct memories of being a less than stellar lover in my teen years."

Macy shrugged. "I guess you're right. College guys weren't much better. They'd probably gotten hold of some sex manuals or something, and they'd had some practice, but they hadn't quite mastered their technique yet."

"I'm hoping your experiences have improved since then."

She smiled, letting her gaze travel down the length of him and back up. "There's definitely been a huge improvement in the past few days."

"You wouldn't just say that to soothe my ego, would you?" he said as he stripped off his clothes.

"You have an ego? I never noticed." The little smile that still played on her lips said otherwise, though.

Griffin had some idea that he could come off as an arrogant bastard at times, and he supposed he looked at it as a way of staying competitive at work. He was confident in himself, and he knew that on the playing field, confidence counted for a lot. Letting the opponent see it often meant gaining the competitive edge.

Problem was, some people didn't consider the workplace a playing field.

Possibly people like Macy. But that's where he had a hard time reading her. Either she knew the game and played it like a pro, using her considerable sex appeal to distract and charm, or she really was just a pretty woman with absolutely no idea how strongly she affected him.

Well, after this weekend, she'd have to have an idea.

He crossed the bathroom and stepped into the hot water. Macy reclined and closed her eyes, either uninterested in the sight of him naked or more interested in the relaxing effects of the hot tub. Too bad he didn't possess her sense of restraint.

"You're tired, aren't you?" he asked.

Her eyes remained closed. "No, just relaxing. I'm actually a little wired from the nightclub."

The crisp scent of peppermint oil rose up from the water, and Griffin inhaled deeply as he sat. He moved over to Macy, his knees brushing hers. She parted her thighs, and he came closer, pulled her against him, pressed his lips to her neck and tasted her where she was still a little salty from dancing.

She moaned softly, her eyes still closed. Her hands slid around his hips, gripped his backside, and pulled him closer still, until his cock was pressed against her.

There was something about Macy when she made love—some restraint that he'd never expected to be there. As if she was holding something back. It could have been some niggling doubt that she could trust him not to tell everyone in the office what they'd done.

Or maybe it was just his imagination. Whatever the case, it left him feeling a little as though he'd failed. And this time, he wanted to see her wild and unrestrained. He wanted to push whatever buttons would make her let loose and be as enthusiastic as he'd imagined she could be.

He lifted her up until his mouth found her breasts,

and he sucked and licked them until she squirmed against him. Dipping his head below the surface of the water, he trailed his tongue down her belly, lifted her hips up, and found her delicious opening. He plunged his tongue into her, sucked her clit, drank her in until he had to come up for air.

And when he broke the surface of the water, he caught a tense expression on her face. "Is something wrong?" he asked after taking a deep breath. He brushed the water off his face and pushed his hair back.

"No," she said, puzzled. "Of course not."

"You look a little stressed."

She frowned. "I do?"

"You're not one of those girls who doesn't like oral sex, are you?"

"Yeah, it's right up there with people who mistreat puppy dogs, and green shag carpeting—the kind of things the world can do without," she said as she rose from the water and pulled him to her again.

In spite of her sarcasm, he got the feeling she was trying to hide something. But then she kissed him, and he decided whatever was going on was all in his head. He needed to get over it, and get on with the task at hand.

But...

The doubt surfaced again as he recalled their first encounter when he'd thought she was faking her orgasm, and he felt his cock going soft. He had to know the truth.

"Am I a bad lover or something? Do I have doggy breath?"

She looked at him as though he'd lost his mind. "Of course not. Why would you say that?"

"You're just giving off this weird vibe."

She dragged her fingernails gently up his back. "The only weird thing going on right now is this conversation. I need less talk and more action."

Her hands traveled over his shoulders, down his chest, and when she gripped his cock, there was no longer a hint of softness.

Rock-hard, baby.

"Honestly," she said, "I can't think of many things I like more than oral sex."

She dropped below the surface of the water, and when she took his cock into her mouth, there were no more doubts. Griffin leaned against the side of the tub, resting his arms on the ledge, losing himself to the incredible feel of heat and water and Macy's mouth.

When she surfaced to catch her breath, Griffin couldn't play cat and mouse any longer. He caught her from behind, claimed her neck with his mouth, eased her against the side of the hot tub, and buried his cock deep inside her. Her delicious wet heat was so similar to the feel of the hot tub, the only difference was the sensation of tightness, and then friction as he moved inside her.

He wanted to hold on to her. And not just in the here and now. He wanted this to be more than a weekend fling.

If he could only get rid of the doubts that plagued him, of the suspicion that Macy was playing him. Well, he'd know the truth soon enough. Returning to the real world would be the true test.

For now, he just wanted to get lost in her.

His fingers spanned the width of her hips as their bodies met. He gripped her and pounded into her, over and over, losing himself in the frenzy of it. The motion of their lovemaking sent water splashing back and forth.

Macy arched her back, gasping as she moved in time with him, coaxing their bodies into a faster and faster rhythm, into a greater and greater frenzy of pleasure as water sloshed out of the tub and the sounds of their lovemaking echoed off the walls.

This, good as it was, wasn't enough. No matter how hard he tried, he couldn't make it enough.

He wanted more from Macy. Maybe more than she was willing to give.

10

MACY HATED seeing the weekend end, but part of her was eager to get back to the office, show the senior partners why she deserved to be creative director, and ultimately get her promotion.

The sad part was seeing her stint as Queen of the Fake Orgasm end…or was that the happy part? She couldn't be sure. After Griffin's hungry, eager love-making, she was left with an odd feeling. As if he wanted something from her.

They had stayed up way too late last night, then slept in this morning and had barely had time to grab coffee at a hotel shop before catching their car to the airport, where Lauren and Carson were already there waiting for them.

They'd said goodbye to Lauren at another gate, and now they were boarded onto their flight back to San Francisco, waiting for the plane to take off. Carson had a seat directly behind theirs, but apparently he'd had a busy night because he was already crashed out, his mouth gaping open, she saw, when she peered at him from between the seats.

Without his prying ears, she felt comfortable saying

to Griffin, "I was hoping we could come to some kind of agreement about going back to work."

"What? You mean when I get the promotion and you don't?" His half smile hinted that he was joking, but Macy wasn't feeling very amused that their plane hadn't even taken off yet and he was already back to his usual asshole-at-work self.

"Don't be so sure of yourself," she said lamely. She hated when he caught her unprepared with a snappy comeback. A few hours from now, when she was in her apartment unpacking her bags, she'd think of the perfect thing to say.

"I'm sorry," Griffin said as he placed a bag of M & Ms he'd bought at the airport on her lap. "I was joking. Please tell me what you were going to say."

"What's with the M & Ms?"

"It's a peace offering. I bought them for you, anyway."

Macy's anger vanished. "You knew in advance that you'd need a peace offering for me?"

"I took a wild guess about what your favorite candy is. Did I get it right?"

"I'm impressed. You're pretty much on the money. My favorite would have to be a tie between these and Snickers."

"I'm a Mounds man myself."

"Aren't you all?"

"Ha. Mounds, breasts, I get it. I didn't even catch that ahead of time. You're good."

"Definitely not one of my better jokes."

"I'm an easy audience. But seriously, what did you

want to talk to me about. Some kind of work agreement?"

"I just want to make sure we have the same expectations, you know, going back to work."

After last night, she was left feeling as though she and Griffin had different expectations. But she couldn't begin to guess what his were. If he was hoping for an office booty-call honey, someone to screw on lunch breaks, he was going to be sorely disappointed. She didn't care how amazing he might be in bed, she wasn't about to compromise her work situation any more than she already had.

"You mean like do we get to boink on lunch breaks, that kind of thing?" he said.

"I don't think we should be doing anymore boinking at all. Do you?"

"I'm a guy. I almost never think I shouldn't be boinking a pretty girl like you."

"Let's be professionals about this, why don't we?"

"Does that mean I can start charging you for sex?"

"Sh!" Macy glanced around. "Someone's going to think you're serious."

"I'll have women lined up outside the restroom every time I need to go to the john."

"I hope we can keep what happened this weekend to ourselves," Macy said.

"Of course. I don't kiss and tell."

"Do you think Carson can keep quiet?"

"Oh, yeah. I've got major dirt on him. He wouldn't think of talking."

"I've had a great time this weekend. Thanks," she said. "I'm a little sad to see it end."

"It doesn't have to."

"It's better if it does. Now that we've cleared the air of all that sexual tension, we should be able to work much more effectively together, don't you think?"

Griffin settled back into his chair, his expression making it clear he didn't quite buy her argument. "It's weird, I was trying to brainstorm a little more on my own this morning on our way to the airport, and it's like my brain is set on low-power mode today or something."

"Sex will do that to you," Macy blurted without thinking.

Well, he didn't know about the study. He couldn't know she was serious.

She looked out the window at the tarmac, where airport employees were busy hurling the passengers' bags onto the plane. Good thing she'd only brought a carry-on.

"No, no, you've got it wrong. It's athletic ability that's supposed to be adversely affected by sex, but I think they've proven that to be an old wives' tale."

"Who's they?" Macy said, glad for the distraction.

"You know, those imbeciles who go around studying the ridiculous minutiae of human behavior."

"You mean scientists."

"If that's what we're calling them these days."

Macy smiled as she imagined what Lauren would think if she witnessed this conversation. Likely her flight attendant persona would disappear in a flash.

"So," Griffin said. "Nervous about the promotion announcement?"

"Do we have to talk about that?"

He shrugged. "Nope."

She dug a book out of her purse, shoved her purse under the seat in front of her, then pretended to be engrossed in her reading. But his head game was working. All she could think about was the promotion.

"Since you asked," she said, snapping her book closed. "No, I'm not nervous at all. What would I have to worry about when I'm going to get the job?"

"Hey, if you're that confident, then nothing."

"Just like you—we're both sure we'll get it. One of us is going to be seriously disappointed."

"Yep," he said, flipping through the in-flight magazine, his lack of concern making it clear who he thought would be disappointed.

Macy studied his game face, knowing she had something to learn from it. Because he was getting to her. She couldn't deny it. She wasn't as good at head games as he was. But she'd learn from the master, and then the student would become the master. Just like in the kung fu flicks she and Lauren secretly loved to watch.

So what would the master do right now? She bit her lip, giving the matter some thought as her fingers traced the embossed lettering on the cover of her historical romance. He'd say, whatever it took to get the upper hand.

And if she really wanted to avoid the possibility of falling into bed with Griffin again, she might as well piss him off good and well. What was the one thing that could piss a guy off, guaranteed?

Insult his manhood.

Griffin's manhood wasn't exactly ripe for insulting,

but she did have one thing on him. She knew his vulnerability, and she had to exploit it.

Macy leaned toward him, putting her mouth close to his ear. He smiled. She exhaled, letting her breath caress his cheek.

"Remember Friday night?" she said, her voice low and sultry.

"How could I forget?"

"When you thought I might be faking it?"

"Yeah."

Macy paused for dramatic effect, watching his smile fade. He looked over at her, confused.

"I was."

GRIFFIN DIDN'T USUALLY let shots below the belt get to him, but Macy had an uncanny ability to find his weak spot and pound it.

"You faked it? Why?"

She shrugged. "I wasn't that excited."

"I beg to differ. What about all that 'umming and ahhing'? You were just acting?"

"I did win an award for it, after all."

"That's pretty low," he said, not sure whether to feel pissed off or impressed by her tactics.

"If it makes you feel better to believe I was having wildly enjoyable sex, feel free. I wouldn't want to shatter your self-image."

He cast a vaguely amused look in her direction.

She couldn't have just said what he thought she'd said.

But she had.

And if her claim of faking it hadn't rung true, he might not have believed her.

"So you faked it every time?"

She shrugged again.

"Did you?"

"Does it matter?" she asked, smiling.

"Why would you want to keep going and going and going if you weren't enjoying yourself that much?"

"I kept hoping it would get better, I guess."

"Are you playing head games with me? Because if you are, you need to do a better job of lying. I don't believe you."

She opened her book and stared at it. "That's okay. Maybe you're right. Maybe I'm lying."

Griffin wanted to kiss the smirk off her face. But they'd agreed no more hanky-panky. Damn common sense. Sometimes he wished he could do without it.

He leaned in close to her now, his mouth nearly touching her ear. "I'm sure you're lying, because you were so hot for me, you couldn't control yourself."

But the truth was, he'd been so hot for her, he could hardly think straight. He might not have been coherent enough to read her every sign. He'd tried, but she turned him into a crazed version of himself when she took her clothes off.

"You're right," she said, too casually. "I'm lying. I came every time. Best sex of my life."

Griffin sat back in his chair again, his victory feeling hollow at best. She was playing head games with him for sure, but his brain was too foggy from a weekend of partying to think very clearly. And he was tired. Damn tired. Fine. Let her have her little victory.

He was going to take a nap. He closed his eyes, but her claim kept echoing in his head.

She was faking it…faking it…faking it.

SUNDAY AFTERNOON roller-skating had been a tradition with Macy and Lauren for the past year, and since their planes had both arrived in the city in the early afternoon, they'd caught up via cell phone and agreed to meet at Golden Gate Park as usual.

Macy had just skated a few warm-up rounds around the makeshift roller rink, and now she was skating in time with the music that was blaring out of nearby speakers, something vaguely familiar by Earth, Wind and Fire, while Lauren checked out the fresh meat skating around the park.

"So you think the promotion is in the bag?" Lauren asked when she could no longer check out the hotties without looking too obvious.

Macy lost her balance for a second, splayed her arms out to each side, and caught herself before she could fall. Was it a coincidence, or did the thought of what she'd done this weekend really throw her so off balance— literally?

She bit her lip and considered Lauren's question. "Hard to say. I mean, Griffin maybe seemed a little fuzzy-headed. I guess we'll have to wait and see how noticeable the effects are at work, right?"

"Oh, believe me, if you rocked his world as much

as you claim you did, you *will* notice the effects. It's a proven fact now, thanks to me."

"Don't look so pleased with yourself. It's obnoxious."

"That's actually the look I was going for," Lauren quipped as she checked out a guy in ripped jeans and a black leather jacket skating past, shaking his hips to the music.

Normally Macy would have found Lauren's ease with her own attitude amusing, but now she couldn't get past the feeling of heaviness that was sitting on her chest, threatening to ruin her satisfaction that she'd accomplished her weekend seduction plan and now had only to wait for the results to show themselves.

She tried to focus on having a little bit of rhythm while skating, but instead she felt as if she was just going through the motions, not really hearing the music.

"What's the matter with you?" Lauren finally asked. "You seem pissed or something."

"Nothing," Macy lied, because she didn't have any good answer. She really didn't know why all of a sudden she felt as though everything had gone wrong.

What if Griffin had taken her overtures too seriously? What if she would be hurting him, just like Lauren might be hurting Carson by never giving him a chance?

"Actually," she said before Lauren could speak again. "I was just wondering about Carson and you. Any chance of anything there?"

"Hell, no."

"You can't hide from him forever," Macy said. "From what he said after we dropped you at your gate, he thinks he *does* have a chance."

"Actually, I think I can hide from him pretty much forever. This is a big city, and I'm only one person."

"How do you think it's going to be for me, having to lie to a friend I work with every day?"

Lauren didn't look overly concerned. "I was hoping you could just get over it."

"What if I can't?" Maybe Macy was being a little unreasonable, but she was feeling crankier by the second.

Sexual deprivation and all. That had to be it.

Lauren spun around to skate backward in front of Macy. "You can be a monumental pain in the ass, you know that?"

"I just don't want to be a party to your lies, that's all."

"So now you're Miss High-and-Mighty? After having sex with a guy just so you could secure your own promotion?"

Something inside Macy snapped.

Lauren had said a lot of things to Macy over the years—things someone who wasn't her best friend couldn't have gotten away with. And she'd always put up with it, because Lauren was usually right.

But this was hitting too close to home. She felt her face burning with something akin to anger, something like embarrassment. Maybe a mixture of both.

"That was low. You're the one who suggested it in the first place."

"And you're the one who went along."

Lauren spun again and skated ahead, and Macy, for once, didn't feel like following after her. Didn't feel like keeping up with someone else's pace.

She stopped, turned and skated the other way, toward her parked car on the side of the street. Her eyes stung, and she was going to have a whole new reason to feel as if she were in junior high again if she started crying like a baby right now. She blinked away tears.

Really, the only reason she was emotional was stress. That's all it was. But Lauren had gone too far, and did Macy need friends who could insult her so casually and so completely without even flinching? Of course she didn't.

But the very thought of not having Lauren in her life left her feeling vaguely empty and unmoored.

She tugged her skates off and tossed them in the trunk, jammed her feet into a pair of pink sneakers, and got in the car. She'd driven on autopilot most of the way home before realizing this was the first real argument she'd ever had with Lauren.

What was it about putting on roller skates that had turned their entire relationship, in the space of a few minutes, into some ridiculous preteen drama? She was back in junior high—which was the only time in her life that was measurably worse than high school.

She couldn't see any easy way to repair this crap with Lauren short of an apology. But Lauren didn't do apologies. At least Macy had never witnessed one.

She parked and went into her apartment, ran up the stairs and went straight to the fridge for emergency caffeine. A lonely can of Mountain Dew sat in the back of the refrigerator for occasions like this, and then she found a bag of peanut M & Ms hidden in her top cabinet. Comfort junk food.

She'd plowed through half the bag when the phone rang, and her first instinct was to ignore it. She let the answering machine pick up, half expecting it to be Lauren calling to curse her out for ditching her at the park.

Instead, it was Carson.

"Hey, Macy," he said to the answering machine. "I was just hoping you'd give in and let me know how I can get in touch with—"

Macy grabbed the phone from the end table, pressed the talk button, and interrupted him. "Carson, hi."

"Screening calls, eh?"

"Kinda sorta." Macy frowned at the bag of candy and felt a surge of guilt over her lack of willpower.

"What's the deal with your friend Lauren? I tried calling the number she gave me and it's a Korean restaurant."

"Oh, it is?"

"Are you going to give me her real phone number or what?"

Macy calculated her options. She could lie, put Carson off and be the one dealing with him for the next six months. He didn't seem like the kind of guy who gave up easily, and she didn't want this driving a wedge between them at the office. Lauren may have come to Vegas to hang with Carson as a favor to her, but Macy hadn't asked her to lie. And she couldn't see how a free trip was any special chore on Lauren's part.

She took a deep breath and let her instincts make the decision.

"You want her number? Here it is," she said, then spouted off the numbers she knew by heart but would probably never need to dial again at this rate.

"Got it," he said, after what she could only assume was a pause to copy the phone number down.

This seemed like an adequate compromise to Macy. She hadn't given up Lauren's true identity— she'd just handed the problem of Carson over to her to deal with. Lauren's answering machine didn't reveal her name, so if she wanted to tell any more of the truth—or if she wanted to keep lying—she could do it herself.

"Please don't use this information to stalk her, okay?"

"Do I seem like a stalker to you?"

Macy made a doubtful noise. "You never know."

"I guess if you get that promotion, you can always fire me if I harass your friend, right? Is her real name even Lauren Smith?"

"So you don't believe Griffin's propaganda that he's a shoo-in for creative director?" Macy asked, suddenly liking Carson even better than before.

He laughed. "Hey, Griffin's biggest strength and his biggest weakness is his confidence. There's such a thing as too much of it."

"True."

"Don't get me wrong, I love the guy and all. I think he'd be great in the job, but I've worked with you, too, and I know you're as capable as he is."

"Are you kissing my ass because I gave you Lauren's number?" Macy stretched out long on the couch, set aside the bag of candy and stared up at the ceiling.

"I'm definitely not ass-kissing. I mean, I've already got the number. What would be the point?"

"Maybe you're digging for further info. Her address, social security number, bra size…"

"Nope. And let me say this, if Griffin's got a problem with overconfidence, you've got the opposite problem. You need to show more confidence if you want the higher-ups to take notice of you."

Macy thought about her shamrock trophy, the emblem of what could happen when she really stepped out and showed confidence in herself. Well, big whoop, she'd won a cheesy plastic trophy in a fake orgasm contest. Really something to be proud of.

"Maybe you've got a point there," she said. "I guess I tend to forget that not everyone knows how brilliant and talented I am."

"Exactly. But, you know, you didn't answer me about Lauren's real name."

"Yes, her name is Lauren. Happy?" Macy said, skipping over the whole last-name issue, praying Carson wouldn't notice.

"Thanks, Macy. I really appreciate this."

"Are you that into her, or is this just a matter of pride? Like you can't be the one who gets dumped?"

"What can I say—I felt a connection. This has nothing to do with being the dumper or dumpee."

"You think she felt the same connection?"

"You're her friend. Are you trying to tell me she didn't?"

"Actually, we may not be friends after today, and frankly, I don't presume to know anything about Lauren's emotional life. She's kind of a closed book."

"Whoa—I hope this fallout thing doesn't have anything to do with you giving me her number. If so, I'll toss it and leave her alone."

Macy bit her lip, weighing the best way to answer. "Don't worry, it has nothing to do with you," she lied.

"Is there anything I can do to help repair things between you?"

"No, we've just had a differing of opinions, that's all."

She said goodbye to Carson and hung up the phone. Then she sat on the couch staring at the instrument, half wishing tomorrow would hurry up and get here so she could see Griffin again, and half wishing she'd never have to see Griffin again.

_11_

"DAMN IT," Griffin muttered to himself as he thumbed through his presentation notes.

He didn't feel as though he was at the top of his game today, when he most needed to be, and it was obvious why. He'd partied hard all weekend instead of conserving his energy and staying focused on the goal at hand. He had a presentation to do this morning for a major account, presenting the creative team's concept for the company's revamped Web site and print media campaign.

He took a long drink of coffee—his fourth cup—but caffeine wasn't going to erase the effects of the weekend completely.

Or the effects of Macy.

Damn it again. He should have known better than to think that one hot weekend with her would dampen his desire for her or eliminate his tendency to be distracted by her at the most inopportune times. Having her in his bed had only amplified her effect on him.

"Hey, Griffin? You okay, man?" Carson was standing in front of Griffin's desk wearing a perplexed expression.

"Yeah, sure," he said, snapping out of his daze.

"You looked like you'd been hypnotized—you were just staring at your coffee mug like you'd never seen one before."

"I'm in a funk from this weekend. Partied a little too hard, I guess."

"I hear you—Lauren rocked my world. Wasn't sure I'd be able to walk upright today, to be honest."

"You think you'll see her again?"

"I sure as hell hope so. She's one wild party girl."

Griffin downed the rest of his coffee and set the cup aside. "Guess we'd better get this presentation rolling, eh?"

"I've already got the multimedia set up and ready to roll. From this point on, you're the man."

"Let's hope so," Griffin said, surprised at his own sudden lack of confidence.

"Dude, you're not sounding like yourself."

"I don't know what it is. It's like, I'm wondering if maybe it was a huge mistake to let things get so out of hand with Macy."

"I'm not arguing with that, but what's done is done. Macy's a cool chick. She's not going to let things get ugly at work."

"But pretty soon, I'm going to be her boss. How's that going to look?"

"It's going to look fine so long as you don't let anything else happen."

"Right," Griffin said without totally feeling it.

Not having Macy again sounded about as appealing as bringing lobster to lunch every day but never being allowed to eat it. Macy was his forbidden lobster.

He walked with Carson to the meeting room, dominated by a gleaming mahogany table with clean modern lines. On the far wall was a large plasma TV for video presentations, and on the opposite wall was a large white board for note-taking and brainstorming sessions. This was the one place where Griffin always felt most in his groove.

He loved having all eyes on him as he laid out ideas, loved the synergy that came from creative minds working together on a project, and he'd known up until today that he was the man for the job of creative director.

So what had changed?

He didn't have to consider the question. Macy was what had changed—changed his perspective, that is.

Was she any less capable than him? Any less deserving of the job?

Probably not. But he'd been with the firm longer, had always made a point of being visible to management, and those two things gave him an edge she didn't have.

Mostly, though, she'd softened his competitive edge. He didn't want this to be a competition between them. He just wished they were after different goals entirely.

As he set up his presentation materials on the table, the clients and the rest of the creative team began trickling into the room. He said hello to the clients and shook their hands, then glanced up and caught sight of Macy. He'd been so busy all morning, this was the first time he'd seen her since the airport yesterday. She didn't look nearly as tired as he felt.

In fact, she looked amazing in a lavender suit with her hair pulled back in some kind of French-twist thing. She caught him staring and offered a little smile, then tilted her head toward the presentation materials and mouthed the words, "Good luck."

After their conversation on the plane, he wasn't sure if she was being sarcastic or sincere. Probably the former, which seriously pissed him off.

The senior partners, Gordon Bronson and Louis Wade, entered the room, probably sitting in on the presentation to get a better handle on Griffin's recent performance. He took a deep breath and exhaled. He'd figured they'd be here, but seeing them drove home the fact that this was probably his final chance to impress them before they chose a creative director.

He had nothing to worry about. The very fact that he was the de facto team leader in the absence of a creative director meant he was pretty much guaranteed the job. All he had to do was stand here and not screw up.

Which normally wouldn't have been a problem. But this morning, with his brain operating on low-power mode, he had a feeling not screwing up was going to be a challenge.

"WHAT THE HELL, man?" Griffin said as he closed the door to the conference room and turned back to Macy and Carson, both still sitting at the table now that the room had cleared out.

"What?" Carson said.

"I'm off my game. Did you see me up there stammering and stumbling like a dumb ass? It's like my brain's moving through quicksand this morning."

Macy shrugged as she fiddled with her pen. "I didn't notice. I thought the presentation went pretty well. Didn't you, Carson?"

"Now that you mention it, you did seem a little like you didn't know what the hell you were talking about a few times."

"That's what I mean—I just blanked out and had to make stuff up to cover. You could have jumped in, you know."

"Sorry, dude. I didn't want to steal your thunder," Carson said. "I know it's all about the promotion this week."

"I did jump in when you were dealing with something I could speak knowledgably about," said Macy. "And really, I think you did just fine."

"After today, they'll probably think they'd be better off giving a monkey the promotion."

"Or Macy," Carson added in his oh-so-helpful-asshole voice.

"Ha-ha," Macy said, shooting him the look of death.

"I'm serious," Carson said, edging out of the range of her fist. "I think you'd be more capable than a monkey for sure. Griffin, I'm not so sure about."

She rolled her eyes. "Why don't we focus on what went right here? You sold the clients on our idea for the Earth Clean campaign, and that's all that matters, right?"

Sure, promotion aside, they had at least accomplished that. In spite of his fumbling presentation, the campaign had pretty much sold itself.

Carson glanced at his watch. "I'd love to stick around for a Griffin-ego-boosting session, but I've got a meeting in twenty minutes. I'm outta here."

As Carson got up and left, Griffin pulled out a chair next to Macy and sat. When the conference-room door closed behind Carson, it was their first time alone together since they'd left the hotel, and he only realized now how badly he was missing the crazy-intense relationship that had sprung up between them in a matter of days.

"Thanks for not making me feel like such a dumb ass," he said.

Macy watched him with a half-lidded gaze, the sort he associated with lazy after-sex mornings. "I thought you did fine. Really."

"You have time this afternoon to work on the Golden Gate presentation with me and Carson?"

"Sure, I think my schedule's clear. Is our deadline still Wednesday?"

Griffin nodded. "I think we've got solid ideas. We just need to fine tune and lay it all out to present."

Macy said nothing for a few moments. A peculiar expression played on her lips, and then when she finally spoke, her voice was low. "This isn't awkward like I thought it would be."

"What, you mean us?"

"Yeah. I just thought… I don't know. I thought I wouldn't like you, and that I'd have to work with this guy I'd slept with but couldn't stand."

"Gee, thanks. Nice to know I give off such great vibes."

She laughed. "You know how it's been between us before this weekend."

"Competitive."

"Exactly."

"That's just me. I don't know how not to be a competitor."

"So everyone's your opponent, including me."

"Well, except when you're not."

"So we're on the same team now?"

"Something like that." He leaned in a little closer, one elbow on the table, conscious that anyone could look in the conference-room window at any moment.

All they'd see were two colleagues talking. They wouldn't see how badly he wanted to lay Macy out on the table and bury his cock deep inside her, strip her out of that stiff suit and lick her tits until his tongue ached, grab hold of her soft, round hips and hold on for dear life. Nor would they see the attraction that nearly hummed in the air between them.

Or at least he hoped they wouldn't.

But so what if they did? That wouldn't be so bad.

"You know," Macy said, "I'm sorry about what I said on the plane yesterday. It was just me trying to gain the competitive edge, I guess."

"Really?"

"I didn't mean it."

Notice she never said that she hadn't faked it.

"Don't give it another thought. I've already forgotten it. I mean, that was all the way back in Vegas."

"And you know what they say," she said, smiling.

"What happens in Vegas—"

"Stays in Vegas."

"Guess it never really works out that way, huh?"

She shrugged, then looked down at her notes from the meeting. He followed her gaze and saw that she'd scrawled a few words, but most of her page was covered with indecipherable doodles.

"Was I that boring?"

"Oh, the scribbling? I always do that. Bad habit. Guess it comes with being in the art department."

"So are we declaring an official peace treaty?" Griffin asked.

"Us, work together in peace? I guess anything's possible," she said, her eyes twinkling.

"Seriously. I want us to have a good working relationship."

She nodded. "Me, too. I think we can handle that."

"Does that mean we can have friendly office-buddy sex?" He blurted, only half joking.

"I don't think that's a good idea, and I really doubt you do."

"Oh, trust me, I do. I mean, it's not like anyone has been promoted yet, and until then…"

"We're free to be sex buddies?"

"That's my theory, yes."

She smiled then, a smile he wasn't sure he could trust. "I'm tempted to say yes, but you already seem like you were adversely affected by this weekend. I don't want to make you any worse off than you already are."

"Hmm, good point. And rather selfless of you, being worried about my job performance this of all weeks."

She shrugged. "I wouldn't call it selfless."

"But I thought you said I did fine in the presentation. Are you implying otherwise now?"

"Oh, um…no. You just seem a little less sharp than usual. Or something."

Or something. She'd screwed him within an inch of his life—that was the problem. And if he didn't know better, he'd have suspected she did it just to make him look bad this week.

MACY DUCKED INTO the restroom and peered under all the bathroom stalls. No one here. Thank God. She was not in the mood to engage in restroom chitchat.

She paced back and forth across the tile floor, her conscience battling with her ambition. It had been painful to watch Griffin fumbling around during the Earth Clean presentation, clearly operating at reduced capacity. She felt like a horrible, horrible person for having put him in that condition on purpose.

But then again, it had been a tiny bit enjoyable, too, to see Mr. Always Perfect screwing up in front of everyone. Minor screw-ups, but still. It was something.

And the fact that she was even pleased with his minor failure made her an even more horrible person.

She stomped into a stall and closed it, then put down the toilet-seat lid and sat on it, while her brain whirred with warring thoughts.

On the one hand, she wanted that creative director promotion so badly she could taste it. She wanted the challenge, the responsibility, the chance to show everyone the extent of her creative talent.

On the other hand, she might never be able to live with herself if she got the promotion unjustly.

That whole sexing-Griffin-out-of-his-brain-power thing had only sounded good to her because—she had to face it—it was an excuse to have sex with him. And maybe she'd wanted that almost as badly as she wanted the promotion.

Which was really pitiful. Total nerd-girl decision making at work there.

Part of her wanted to even the playing field now by sleeping with him again, this time letting herself lose her own share of IQ points. That way, they'd be on equal footing at work.

But she knew in her heart that was just further justification for sleeping with her adolescent-fantasy guy.

And so the fair thing to do, the right thing to do, would be to make up for what she'd done by helping Griffin look good at work.

Maybe she owed him even more than that, though. Maybe she had to step out of the running for the creative director job if she really want to make up for her crappy behavior. But that thought made her stomach lurch and sweat break out on her upper lip. She nearly lost her balance on the toilet and had to brace her hands against the walls of the stall.

She couldn't go that far right now. But she had to consider it seriously. And soon.

"Damn it," she muttered.

Sometimes doing the right thing really, really sucked the big one.

12

EVEN THOUGH they'd called that truce, Griffin had still been surprised at how cooperatively Macy had worked with him ever since. It had almost been as if she were trying to make him look good in front of everyone else.

It was bizarre, given their history.

They'd sailed through two days without the slightest bit of tension, and by Wednesday, his foggy-headed stupor had gone and he'd been feeling sharper than ever for the Golden Gate presentation, which, with Macy's and Carson's help, they'd aced.

If he hadn't been mistaken, he was pretty damn sure they'd blown away the senior partners, too.

All in all, a good week's work. But now it was Friday afternoon, and still no announcement had been made regarding the promotion.

Griffin answered some e-mail, filed some papers, then glanced at his watch. It was almost five o'clock. His gut twisted at the notion that another day—or another weekend—would pass without knowing he'd gotten the promotion. At that thought, he looked across the room to where Macy stood talking to the receptionist.

How would his getting the job affect their relationship? He'd always imagined Macy as a fierce competitor in the workplace, but now that he knew her in her off hours, she didn't seem so fierce. In fact, she was hardly the woman he'd built her up to be in his head. Gone was the image of a coy vixen using her charms against him, replaced by a soft, funny, vulnerable, intelligent woman whom he was falling for harder by the day.

No denying it. He didn't want to play it casual with Macy. She wasn't his idea of a weekend fling. She was the kind of woman he wanted to spend more time getting to know. Not that she was interested, but still. A guy could dream.

As if she could feel him watching her, she glanced in his direction and smiled when their gazes met. She was wearing a sexy pink suit today, with something silky and white peeking out from between the jacket lapels. Probably one of those lace camisoles she so often wore, the ones that made him want to strip her naked and lick her all over.

He smiled back, and it occurred to him only then that she was probably just as anxious as he was to hear the decision about the job. In fact, she'd been pacing the office all day, making trips to other people's desks, to the copy machine, to the break room, as if she couldn't sit still—

His phone rang. He picked it up and said hello.

"Hey, Grif, can you come down to my office right now?" It was Gordon Bronson's voice, and he didn't sound like he had bad news.

Exhilaration shot through Griffin's body. This was it. The news they'd all been waiting for.

"I'll be there in a sec," he said.

He hung up the phone and caught Macy's eye again as he stood. He wanted this good news to be something they could celebrate together, but it would only be good news for one of them. Not exactly the recipe for relationship bliss.

Macy looked back to the receptionist, who was talking about something exciting judging by the wild flailing of her hands, and Griffin headed for the senior admin offices. Through the window of Gordon's office, he could see the partners talking, and he fought to keep his smile from showing too soon.

The admin assistant waved him straight into Gordon's office.

"Please have a seat," Louis Wade said.

No sooner had Griffin taken a seat on the plush visitors' sofa than both men said, "Congratulations."

He looked from one man to the other, and they put him out of his misery. "We'd like to offer you the creative director position," Gordon said.

Before Griffin could respond, Louis cut in. "We've considered all the applicants carefully, and based on your seniority, level of experience and impressive performance, we all agree that you're the man for the job."

"Thank you," Griffin said, trying not to beam too much. "I'm honored to take the position, and I'll do my best to exceed your expectations."

God, he sounded like such a brownnoser, but he couldn't help it. He really was grateful for the chance to take the job. He'd been grooming himself for it since the day he'd started at the agency, and this promotion marked the culmination of his greatest career goal. It marked the chance for him to feel like he finally had the freedom to make decisions, to spearhead creative efforts, to go with his own vision instead of following someone else's.

He'd been aching for that kind of challenge for years.

"You'll assume the new position on Monday, if that works for you."

"Absolutely."

"And we'll be interviewing for your replacement. Once he or she is hired, you'll be responsible for overseeing their training. Do you have any questions?"

Griffin definitely had questions about the compensation package, but he figured that could wait. "Will an announcement about this be made to the office, or should I gather up the creative department and let them know myself?"

"We'll make a formal announcement first thing Monday, but if you'd like to give your department a heads-up now, feel free."

Griffin stood up, nodding. He shook each senior partner's hand and thanked them for the opportunity.

And as soon as he was out the door, he wondered how the hell to tell Macy. He wanted to be the one to break the news to her. It only seemed fair, after everything they'd been through together.

But how would she react? And how would the news affect their relationship?

She was a fair, mature woman, so while he could imagine she'd be disappointed, he had to believe she'd also be happy for him. And maybe she'd want to help him celebrate the accomplishment once she'd had time to let the news sink in.

When he left the admin office area, he spotted Macy heading toward her desk, and he quickened his pace to catch up with her. A low whistle caught her attention. She turned and spotted him, then stopped and smiled tentatively.

She knew something was up.

"Hey, do you have a few minutes?" he asked.

"Sure, what's up?"

He nodded toward an empty conference room, and she followed him into it. Once they were alone with the door closed, he motioned toward a chair, then took one himself.

"What's up is, I just talked to Bronson and Wade—"

"You got the promotion," she said, smiling. "Congratulations."

Griffin studied her expression, trying to read any tension that might have been behind it. "You're not upset?"

Her smile was wide and genuine. "You earned it. I had a feeling you'd be the one chosen, so it's not exactly a surprise."

"You had just as much chance of getting the job as I did. In the end, I think it came down to seniority. The partners have always been big on company loyalty, and with everything else being equal, I'm guessing they chose me simply because I've been here a few years longer than you have."

Macy's smiled waned a bit. "Don't sell yourself short, okay? And you don't have to couch the news in compliments."

"I wasn't trying to."

"I'm a big girl. I can take it."

Griffin could see a bit of brittleness behind her smile now. Maybe she just needed time to process the news, come to terms with it, and then they'd be cool.

"Are we okay? I mean, us, outside of work?"

A crease formed between her eyebrows. "Griffin, you're my boss now. I just don't think it would be smart for us to continue, you know?"

This is what he'd been most afraid of. This whole you're-my-boss problem.

He winced. "Look, I'm not officially your boss until Monday. Can we at least go out for dinner tonight and talk about this a little more?"

She shook her head and tried to stand, but he caught her wrist gently in his hand and flashed his most hang-dog expression.

"Please? I'd really like to have at least this one last night with you, if nothing else just to smooth out our relationship so we can get a fresh start next week."

But that was a lie, he knew. He wanted the time with her just to have her.

"What exactly needs smoothing out?"

"You know, stuff. Just give me one more night with you, okay?"

One more night and one more day and one more night after that and…

"Let me think about it. I've got a kickboxing class

right after work, and I'll call your cell if I decide we can meet up later."

He nodded. "I'll be here for a while, so if you don't reach my cell, try my work number."

"And if you don't hear from me by seven, you'd better just eat on your own."

Ouch. He suddenly feared he'd be eating lots of meals alone, if he couldn't find a way to keep Macy in his life outside of work.

"If I don't hear from you by seven, I'm calling you," he said, grinning. But he meant it. He wasn't going to let her weasel out of the tough conversation.

She glanced at her watch. "I've got to go."

They said goodbye, and Griffin watched as she walked out the door, hoping like hell this wasn't the death blow to his chances with Macy.

THANK GOD for kickboxing. Macy delivered a side kick to the punching bag, then another and another. She'd been warming up for fifteen minutes, and slowly but surely the tension was draining from her body.

She'd dropped out of the running for the creative director job, so there was no reason she should have been upset over the news that Griffin had gotten the job.

Except she *was* upset. Maybe because she'd shot herself in the foot with that stunt in Las Vegas. Maybe because she'd compromised herself and her chances of getting the promotion.

Or maybe just because she didn't want Griffin to be her boss, since she still wanted him.

Stupid adolescent fantasies.

Lauren, to whom Macy hadn't talked all week and wasn't really keen on talking to now, was watching her kick the hell out of her punching bag from a few feet away. They might have had an argument, but there wasn't really any getting around the fact that they attended the same kickboxing class.

Lauren had stopped her own kicks and moved over to hold Macy's bag. "You look like you want to kill someone," she said.

"I don't want to talk about it."

"Ohhh. It's the promotion, isn't it? Let me guess— Griffin got it?"

"I said…" She paused as she delivered a kick that jarred her all the way to her teeth. "I don't want to talk about it."

"You gave it your best shot. Maybe it's time to ask for a raise, even let them know you'll be looking at other companies if they can't give you some incentive to stick around." Lauren started working through the warm-up again, but only half-heartedly.

"I'm not going to strategize my next career move with you, of all people."

"What's that supposed to mean?"

"It means, your last piece of advice was dubious at best."

"So you're pissed about your plan to dumb him down with sex failing?"

"No, I've just learned not to listen to you."

Lauren rolled her eyes and started to say something else, but then she stopped and shook her head. All of a sudden she was paying attention to the instructor and acting like she was into the whole kickboxing thing, which generally was not the case. She usually showed up mainly to watch the guys, not to work out.

Whatever, Macy thought. Let her be pissed off. Because Macy was still good and pissed off at her.

And it was easier to be mad at Lauren right now than to examine her own motives and what the hell it was that she really wanted out of life.

Forty-five minutes later, Macy was drenched in sweat, and every major muscle group ached as if she'd just endured a heavyweight fight.

She went to the women's locker room without talking to Lauren, then showered while trying to decide whether or not she should have dinner with Griffin. On the one hand, this was her last chance to be with him before he was officially her boss.

On the other hand, if being with him meant feeling even crappier than she did now, she wasn't sure she could handle it.

By the time she was toweling off, she decided she had to give him tonight, maybe even come clean about what she'd done if she was feeling brave, and then they were through. Whatever attraction there was between them—they'd just have to get over it. Which probably wouldn't be hard for Griffin if she could summon the nerve to confess to him.

She dressed, then found her cell phone in her locker and called Griffin.

"Hey, you ready for dinner?" he answered without bothering with greetings.

"Where do you want to meet?"

"Do you know that Indian place with the red walls on Market?"

"Sure. What time?"

"Seven-thirty?"

Macy looked at the clock on the wall overhead. That gave her fifteen minutes to dry her hair and put on makeup. Doable.

"I'll see you there," she said as an impending sense of doom settled in her belly.

She disconnected the call and put the phone in her purse. She had to tell him the truth.

Or did she? Could she live with herself knowing she'd tried to play such a dirty trick on her competition? Would he even believe her if she told him what she'd done?

No, without Lauren's study being public knowledge yet, there was just no freaking way he'd be able to accept that she'd robbed him of some of his IQ points.

More important than the fact that he wouldn't believe her, though, was the fact that she could not bear to face his disillusionment with her. She might have started out having truly crappy motives, but ultimately she'd realized that she wanted to sleep with Griffin because she was attracted to him…but would he buy that? No way. He'd only focus on the bad part, and he'd never respect her again.

She needed his respect not only because of her own ego, but also because he was going to be her boss.

It was definitely best if she just kept quiet about that whole dumb-him-down-with-sex part.

Macy dried her hair quickly, going with messy

waves as her style simply because it was the only thing her hair could do without a curling iron and an extra half hour. She applied a little concealer, mascara, blush and lipstick, and then she grabbed her gym bag and headed for the door.

Twenty minutes later, she'd accomplished the nearly impossible, landing a prime parking spot right in front of the restaurant. She'd worked herself into a bundle of tensed-up muscles, undoing any good that the workout might have done for her stress level. When she passed the restaurant's front window, she saw that Griffin already had a table for them.

When she entered, he smiled and waved.

"I hope you don't mind, I ordered a chai for you," he said when she sat.

"No, that's perfect. It's getting cold outside. I could use something to take the chill off."

Stupid small talk was the last thing she wanted to engage in right now. If he pursued the weather topic any longer, she'd know he shared her sense of doom.

"I'm glad you came," Griffin said.

Okay, so maybe she was the only doomsayer.

"I'm buying tonight, by the way," she said. "It's my way of saying congratulations on your promotion."

"Thank you," he said, smiling again. "I was really worried that this might come between us—that's actually what I want to talk to you about tonight."

Macy took a sip of the chai, which had just barely cooled enough to drink, and she was treated to the spicy-sweet flavor of India.

"Maybe we should eat first," she said.

"Except I've already brought it up, and if we wait, it's going to hang in the air between us and we'll expend all our energy trying to ignore it."

"I just don't want us to argue or get upset, that's all. Not before I've eaten," she added as a joke, but it fell flat. Maybe this wasn't exactly the time to do her stand-up routine.

"That must mean you're preparing to drop the relationship ax."

Macy winced at his directness. "No, but whatever happened to 'this is just a weekend thing,' and 'what happens in Vegas stays in Vegas'?"

"I guess we proved that saying wrong."

"I think it's meant more as a guiding principle, and we're forgetting to follow it." She turned her attention back to her chai, which was much easier to deal with than this conversation.

A waiter conveniently arrived at that moment, and Macy didn't need to look at the menu to know she wanted chicken curry. Once they'd placed their orders and the waiter had left, Griffin pinned her with one of his too-direct stares.

"I don't really care how this relationship started out. All I know now is that I like spending time with you outside of the office, and I want us to figure out if there's a way we can make that happen without it negatively affecting our work life."

He reached for her hand, and she was powerless to pull it away. She stared at his large, capable hand covering hers, and she cursed herself for being such an idiot. Even if he wasn't her boss as of Monday, he would still be the guy she'd been unforgivably dishonest with.

"You know that's not possible."

"Why isn't it?"

"What happens if the relationship ends, then we're stuck working together. It's inevitably going to be awkward if there are feelings involved. And if the relationship doesn't end, you're still my boss, and there's always going to be that perception of impropriety by everyone else in the office. I think it's a road we need to exit right now, before we get too lost."

Griffin didn't attempt to hide his disappointment. "That's not what I was hoping you'd say." He smiled then, but it was filled with melancholy.

And that's when Macy knew she was doing the right thing not to string him along any further. When a relationship was based on lies, the best thing was to end it before it got any more complicated.

"I'm sorry. I want us to continue working together, and I don't regret our having gotten to know each other better outside of work. At least we can work together now without being at each other's throats all the time."

"True. I guess when you look at it like that, this was a good thing while it lasted, right?"

"Absolutely."

"I really do think you deserved the promotion at least as much as I did, maybe more," Griffin said.

"Ditto. But really, the senior partners know what they're doing."

"They sure as hell *think* they do."

"I bet you'll find them a lot easier to deal with, now that you're management."

"We'll see. Have you ever thought of going else-where—someplace you'd have a chance of moving up faster?"

Macy shrugged. She wasn't sure it would be smart to discuss career strategies with her new boss.

"I'm asking you this as a friend, not as a colleague. I think your talents will go to waste if you're not being challenged and recognized."

"I'm sure you'll see to it that I'm challenged and recognized for my accomplishments."

Griffin shook himself. "That just sounds crazy. I guess I was so busy working toward the promotion, I kind of overlooked the fact that it also means becoming the entire creative department's boss."

"Yep, you're the man now," Macy said, smiling.

"Does that mean no one's going to want to be friends with me now?"

"I think it means you have to play golf on Saturday mornings with all your important business associates, and yeah, you probably can't be every-one's best pal."

His brow furrowed. "That kind of sucks."

"Not really. We'll all pretend we really like you. It's only when you're not around that we'll complain about what a slave driver you are."

He made a face at her, and she laughed.

"I've always wanted to have more autonomy, more creative control, but I guess I've never really thought of myself as a company man, you know?"

"So you want the responsibility, but you don't want to be the Man?"

"Maybe, something like that. I don't know. I'm just freaking out is all."

"You're going to be great. You know you will."

"Carson's one of my best friends. How's he going to feel about working for me?"

"I'm sure he'll constantly be using it as an angle to get one over on you."

"That pretty much sounds right."

"I'll try to be more subtle, however," Macy said, but it was so untrue, she hoped he wouldn't believe it even for a second. "You know I'm joking, right?" she added.

"You may say you are, but..."

"Oh, so you don't trust me?"

He grinned. "Should I?"

"Probably not," Macy said, wishing she wasn't serious.

His gaze turned warmer somehow, and she recognized the change as Griffin going into seduction mode. Crap. She wasn't exactly mentally equipped to resist the way she used to be.

"You know... No one has to know if we aren't exactly proper coworkers after hours. I'd never tell. Don't you think we're mature enough to keep the emotions in check?"

Macy tried to do just that. She tried not to let any emotions cloud her judgment. She tried to consider his words evenly, let them seep into her consciousness without reacting. But one little voice in her head said go for it, while another said no way.

"I don't know," she said. "Aren't those just ratio-nalizations?"

"I think they're the truth. I mean, we can deal with it, Macy. I'm sure we can. I can be a fair supervisor. I can separate our private lives from the office."

"I know you *think* you can, but—"

"But sometimes we can't anticipate how it will really play out, I know."

"And how can you not think the responsible thing to do is to end this now? Which head are you thinking with, Griffin?"

"Maybe with you, I always have a little of the wrong-headed thinking going on, but one thing I know for sure is, the chemistry between us is worth explor-ing. I wouldn't set something this powerful aside just out of respect for other people's rules."

Macy felt a jolt from his words. *Something this pow-erful...* He at least had that part right, for sure. She'd never felt such an intense attraction before.

Maybe once she'd decided to break the rules in the first place by seducing Griffin, she'd set out on the path where they'd have to make up the rules as they went along.

And if they got to make up the rules...they might never be able to keep their hands off each other again.

OUTSIDE, the cool night breeze whipped at Macy's hair and made her glad she'd worn a jacket. Griffin held her hand as they walked along the sidewalk past mostly closed businesses, and that simple intimate contact left her feeling warmer all over.

Macy wasn't exactly accustomed to making up rules as she went along. The whole Las Vegas thing had been a big departure for her in the rule-breaking department.

And one self-made rule was for sure. Tonight, Macy was incapable of faking it.

She watched sadness play across Griffin's face in the half darkness as he probably tried to accept that they might have no future together, and she knew she had to give him this weekend. No matter how stupid it might be, she had to give him all of herself if that's what he wanted.

She owed it to him.

But who was she kidding? She wanted him at least as badly as he wanted her, if for no other reason than she finally wanted to have real, no-holds-barred, no-more-faking-it sex with him, after the torture of last weekend.

Well, except torture wasn't the right word. She'd been amazed at how much she'd enjoyed making their lovemaking all about Griffin's pleasure, in spite of his best efforts. Keeping the focus off herself had taught her some interesting things about physical pleasure. Most importantly, that there was as much to be found in giving someone pleasure as there was in receiving it.

Sure, she'd understood that on an intellectual level before, but this little experiment had given her a concrete illustration of its truth.

After dinner, they'd decided to drop in on a little blues club down the street that Macy had heard was featuring a band she liked. As they walked hand in hand the three blocks from the Indian restaurant to the jazz club, taking in the brisk night air, Macy's brain bounced from one idea to the next, as unable to focus as she had been lately.

She wanted to do the right thing with Griffin, but wasn't sure what that was. She was pretty sure sleeping with him again wasn't the right thing, but she wanted to do that as much as she wanted to be virtuous. Her brain bounced around some more as she tried to imagine what it would be like to have Griffin as her boss.

She couldn't think straight, and she wasn't even the one who'd gotten to come. Damn Lauren and her stupid study.

A side effect Lauren apparently wasn't aware of was the very unpleasant inability to focus that came with sexual frustration. Maybe she should have called her research, *You're Damned if You Do and Damned if You Don't.*

It was just like a scientist to pursue some esoteric study while ignoring the obvious facts. Lauren was intelligent and all, but the woman had a serious case of brainiac syndrome—too smart for her own good. And in this case, too smart for everyone else's good as well.

Macy could have lived her life just fine without knowing the truth about sex and its impact on her intelligence.

There was a short line at the entrance of the club. They stopped and waited, and after a moment Macy realized Griffin was staring at her.

"You look like you're busy trying to think up a solution to world hunger," he said.

She smiled, embarrassed at the truth. "Nothing nearly so important."

"What's up?" he asked.

"It's nothing, really."

"It must be something, because I was just talking to you and you didn't hear me."

"Oh." Crap. "Sorry."

"Tuning me out again?"

"Not at all. I'm just…a little upset over a falling-out I had with Lauren, I guess."

"It's okay."

She smiled up at him, and her breath caught in her throat at how handsome he was. Sometimes she took it for granted, because she saw him around the office so much. But tonight, in the light from the streetlamps, with his dark hair swept back, his olive skin aglow and his haunting gray eyes fixed on her, he looked exactly like one of the brooding romance-novel heroes she'd always imagined she'd find someday.

If only for tonight, she could pretend….

"Since when did you need someone to listen when you're talking, anyway," she teased.

"Do I really come across that full of myself?"

"No, you just don't seem to need anyone's input to be sure of your ideas."

"I didn't realize I had to ask to receive. I've always figured people would speak up if they had a problem with what I was saying or if they wanted to challenge me."

Macy was feeling like a bigger and bigger jerk by

the second. "You always sound so sure of yourself, I've just assumed you had your mind made up, and when other people do challenge your ideas, you often argue with them."

He shrugged. "I don't consider it arguing—more like debating. I figure if anyone's ideas are really good, they'll stand up to being questioned."

"Some of us don't operate that way. I mean, I don't really like to argue or debate or whatever you want to call it."

"Yeah, I guess I forget that. Sorry."

"No, I'm the only one who should be apologizing. I promise to listen all the time—no more spacing out."

Macy felt her cheeks burning as they paid their cover charge and entered the dark, noisy club to find a table. She realized the real reason she'd always tuned Griffin out was that she was afraid of liking him. Not listening to him meant not discovering any more about him and not viewing him as a person she could spend some serious time getting to know.

The club was mostly full already, so they found a table for two at the back of the room. On stage, the warm-up act was already playing, and it was nearly impossible to talk over the sound of the music.

Griffin leaned toward her and said into her ear, "No apologies. I can think of plenty of ways for you to make it up to me later tonight. Deal?"

She slid her hand up his thigh, loving the solid feel of him. When her fingertips reached the junction of his thigh and hip, she stopped. "Deal."

He scooted his chair next to hers and draped his arm

over the back of her chair, then leaned in and kissed her cheek gently. The gesture was so intimate, so sweet, she got a lump in her throat.

It was crazy how a weekend could change things. Crazy how, a few weeks ago, she would have laughed out loud if anyone had suggested she'd soon be sitting in a blues club acting lovey-dovey with Griffin. Well, and not even acting, but actually enjoying his company. Maybe even loving it.

Crazy.

The warm-up act finished their final number, and a waitress, a woman named Leta who had waited on Macy before, arrived to take their drink orders. She was tall and dark brown, and she wore her hair in cornrows that hung almost to her waist.

"Hi, Leta," Macy said. "I'll have a bottle of Perrier."

Griffin shot her a suspicious look. "What, you're going to get me drunk and have your way with me while you're perfectly sober?"

"Something like that."

When she was gone, he nudged Macy with his elbow. "So much for my plan to get you drunk and have my way with you."

"I thought you said that was my plan."

"I was just trying to distract you from the truth."

"You don't need to get me drunk," she said.

His gaze was half-lidded, and he was looking at her the same way he did after they made love. As if he knew all her secrets. That gaze unnerved her most of the time, but this time it warmed her, left her feeling breathless and light-headed.

"Why are you looking at me like that?" she asked.

"Because you're full of surprises. I always thought I had you pegged."

"Do I even want to know how you had me pegged?"

"Probably not," he said, looking a little chagrined.

She kept staring at him until he elaborated.

"Okay, okay. I had you labeled a vixen, completely aware of your effect on men and willing to use it to get whatever you wanted."

"Ouch. Did I really come across like that, or are you just that bad at judging people's character?"

"Maybe a little of both."

She smiled. "So you thought this about me and were totally willing to sleep with me, anyway? What's up with that?"

"Um, I'm a guy?"

She shrugged. "I guess it's fair, if you thought I was using sex to get ahead, that you just take advantage of what I was offering."

As soon as the words left her mouth, she regretted them. She then realized just how true they were, only not exactly in the way Griffin had thought.

Using sex to get what she wanted.

"I wasn't giving you credit," he said, "for being the kind of woman who really doesn't understand the effect she has on men."

"What effect is that?" Macy asked, trying her best to sound genuinely curious.

The truth was somewhere in between. Sure, she knew sex could be a weapon, but she'd never quite shed that shy, chubby teenager at her core. Any confidence in herself she showed the world was really just overcompensation.

"It's damn hard to concentrate on work when you're around."

"It is?"

"You know, men are pretty much ruled by their desires. We try our best to keep them in check, but when we're presented with our favorite dish, we can't help but salivate."

"Your work performance doesn't seem to have suffered for my presence."

"Well, it's been a Herculean effort, trust me," he said, grinning. "There have been plenty of times when I've lost my train of thought after getting a glimpse of you, especially when you're wearing a skirt or a low-cut top. I guess I do a decent job of recovering."

"Definitely. I never would have guessed you could be done in by a glimpse of my knees."

Macy wasn't sure she believed his story, but it was flattering nonetheless. She supposed she'd always wanted to be one of those women men lost their minds over, and maybe it was possible she'd become that kind of woman without even realizing it.

That would be her luck.

"I could be done in by all sorts of glimpses of you. So just be careful, okay? No flashing me during important meetings."

Macy laughed as the Harry Yusef Band took the stage. They immediately kicked into a soulful tune about being cleansed by the rain, and conversation was impossible.

Which was a good thing. Macy wasn't sure she needed any more revelations about herself or Griffin or the ever-more-perplexing nature of their attraction to each other.

13

BACK AT HER APARTMENT, Macy felt as if someone had infused her with a superhuman sense of confidence. She'd tried not to put too much stock in Griffin's comments about her effects on men, but somehow, the idea that she was a sexual being to be reckoned with had seeped into her consciousness in a big way.

She barely felt like herself tonight. Instead she felt like a sex goddess, a woman whose sexuality could bring men to their knees and who wasn't afraid to go after exactly what she wanted.

Maybe the sex goddess had been lurking inside her all the time, just crying out to break free. That could certainly explain Macy's willingness to go forward with her plan to seduce Griffin.

Seducing Griffin. How could she reconcile the way she felt right now, so sexy and confident, with the way she'd behaved in Las Vegas? She'd been a woman who'd used *sexy* and *confident* to manipulate and deceive. She'd been the kind of woman she'd never imagined herself being, but in a bad way. In a ruthless willing-to-do-anything-to-get-ahead kind of way.

She'd taken sexuality and confidence and used them for evil.

She stared into the bathroom mirror, not sure, all of a sudden, if she really liked what she saw. And the longer she stared, the more confused she became.

How could she have gotten herself into this? How could she be here now with a guy whose affection for her was based on lies?

It was stupid. It was nasty. It was unconscionable.

And she was becoming a worse person by the second by not putting a stop to this before it went any further.

There was a knock at the bathroom door. "Macy? Are you okay in there?"

She tried to speak, but nothing came out. Her throat tightened, and she expelled a strange little grunt.

"Macy? Are you okay?"

What to say? *Oh, sorry, I just changed my mind. I know you're naked with a full-on erection and I'm supposed to be retrieving birth control in here, but, um, I changed my mind. Let's just be friends, okay?*

Not only was that unfair, but there was no way she'd be willing to say it. She wanted him too much.

She heard the doorknob turn, and then the door opened. She looked over at Griffin, and he saw what must have been her forlorn expression as she stood there naked in front of the mirror.

"What's wrong?" he asked.

No way could she tell him now. Not while he was completely naked, his erection jutting out, his body a monument to male perfection. She wanted him at least as much as he wanted her, and she could only hope the fairest thing to do would be to just give herself over to him completely.

No more holding back. No more sex with a hidden agenda. No more faking it.

"Oh, nothing," she said. "Nothing's wrong. I was just feeling a little…I don't know. A little worried that we're in too deep, if that makes any sense."

He crossed the granite-tile floor and pulled her against him. He felt so warm and so right. So just what she needed right now, from his hard cock against her belly to his capable hands sliding over her backside.

"I'm not in nearly deep enough," he said with a little smile.

"I just mean, I wish I didn't like this—like us—so much. It would make the whole promotion-and-working-together thing a lot easier, don't you think?"

"Let's work on hating each other tomorrow, okay? I've got a different project in mind tonight."

He lifted her up onto the cold tile countertop and wedged himself between her thighs. She wrapped her legs around him, edging closer until their bodies were nearly joined. When she handed him a condom, he gave her a long, slow, toe-curling kiss that erased her doubts.

He put on the condom and pulled her closer, kissed her again, devoured her. His mouth on her mouth, her ears, her neck, her breasts, all in a frenzy. She bit into his shoulder gently, and when he plunged into her, she cried out, nearly delirious with the relief of it.

Like water on her fire.

He thrust all the way into her, backed off, then pushed deeper still. The sensation of her body opening up to him and joining with his created a delicious burning from deep within.

She matched his intensity, propelling them higher, her breath quick and her body tense. She heard herself crying out his name, lost in him, and she felt as if she was going to come before they'd even gotten started.

He felt so incredible as he stretched her body, invaded her. As their flesh slapped together, she could feel her orgasm coming on so fast, there was no way to stop it.

Her gaze locked on his, and he was in the same predicament as her, she could tell. His brow furrowed, his expression transformed by pleasure, he was lost in it, too.

First came the build-up, like a tornado racing toward where their bodies met. Then came the crash as it struck. And their bodies, so exquisitely joined, were the wreckage, bucking together and swirling in the storm of sensations.

Griffin pulled her closer as he spilled himself into her, as her own orgasm passed, and he kissed her, then breathed into her ear, "You're amazing."

"So are you," she whispered back.

He lifted her from the bathroom counter and carried her out into the main room, to the sofa. There, he stretched out beside her, and she never wanted him to move.

Lauren's words echoed in her head then. *The wilder the sex, the more dramatic the results.*

If that was true, she was in deep, deep trouble.

MACY DIDN'T normally spend Saturday mornings lazing around in bed. She liked to get up, clean her apartment, go to the park, have lunch out with friends. That is, when she wasn't working overtime. She probably should have been working this morning, but when her new boss was lying in bed beside her, it was hard to muster any guilt that she wasn't busting her ass over the Golden Gate account.

They'd slept late, gotten up to take a shower, made love in the shower, and then returned to bed with cups of coffee and toasted bagels that sat half-eaten on the nightstand, because halfway through breakfast they'd gotten a little carried away with a game of footsie.

It was almost eleven when the phone rang, and a glance at her caller ID made Macy's stomach lurch. It was her mother calling. She remembered in a horrible rush all the messages her mom had left on her answering machine and her cell phone since last weekend, and how she'd forgotten to return any of the calls.

Well, she hadn't exactly forgotten so much as she'd procrastinated for too long. Now she was in for the mother of all guilt trips, pun intended.

She hated being one of those women who had a dysfunctional relationship with her parents, but there it was. For as long as she could remember, she'd wanted to have one of those mothers she could confide in over coffee, one of those fathers she could have heartfelt conversations with after friendly tennis matches. Instead, she had the modern-day version of Fred and Wilma Flintstone for parents.

"Aren't you going to answer that?" Griffin asked, glancing up from the newspaper he'd retrieved from her front door earlier.

"No, I don't think so." She watched the phone as it rang.

After five rings, the answering machine picked up, and Macy's canned recording blared through a speaker instructing the caller to leave a message.

"Macy, it's your mother, Joy Thomaston. I guess you're too busy to call me back, so I'll stop calling. You call if you ever have time for your own mother." Then she hung up.

Eek.

"She has to tell you her full name?" Griffin asked.

"That's her version of sarcasm. My mom's not quite right in the head. Actually both my parents are kind of whacked."

"Oh come on, they can't be that bad."

Macy looked out her bedroom window. The sky was a shocking, crisp blue, something that always gave her a surge of energy and a renewed sense of purpose. But at the moment, with Fred and Wilma on her mind, it just made her want to bury her head under the pillow and wait for nighttime, when it would be too late to call her parents.

"Yes, they can. They mean well, but they're just not... I don't know. They're clueless."

"You wouldn't be normal if you didn't hate your parents."

"That's not true. I have friends with wonderful parents, parents they can't wait to spend time with."

"Then your friends are the ones who're screwed up."

"So what's so bad about your parents?"

Griffin stretched his arms over his head, and Macy couldn't help but admire his perfectly sculpted chest and biceps.

"They're just a little uptight. We get along fine, so long as I'm successful by their standards, which are pretty damn high."

"Then they'll be thrilled to hear you got the promotion."

"They'll want to know why I'm not a partner at the firm yet."

"So they pushed you a lot?"

"Oh, yeah. I had to be the best at every sport, have the highest grade-point average, get scholarships to the best schools…."

"Sounds like loads of fun. You should have lived at my house. My mom would have just fed you a brownie and told you to go take a nap instead of worrying about your homework."

He laughed. "At my house, there were no brownies. Only high-fiber bran muffins."

"Yum."

"Don't you think you ought to just call your mom and get it over with? If you don't, you'll stress about it all day."

"Will not."

"You will. I can tell by the way you've been acting ever since the phone rang."

Macy sighed and admitted defeat. He was right, of course. Best to get the dreaded task out of the way.

She grabbed the phone, dialed the number she knew by heart, and waited. A few hundred miles away in Fresno, her mother picked up the phone and said, "Hello."

"Hi, Mom. You called a little while ago?"

"Are you screening calls again, Macy?"

"I was in the shower," she lied.

"Where were you last weekend? I left six messages, I tried your cell phone and you never called back."

"Sorry, Mom. I had a business trip, and I was just so busy, I didn't think to check my messages."

"You must have checked them when you got home." Her mother's voice had taken on the dreaded accusatory tone, the one that had succeeded in inducing major guilt for as long as Macy could remember.

"I did, but you didn't sound like you were calling about anything urgent, and it's been a crazy-busy week. I'd planned on calling you today."

Silence. Her mother was a master at employing the silent treatment, especially over phone lines.

Luckily, Griffin was there to provide her entertainment during the intermission. He draped his leg over hers and traced his fingers along her hipbone, then across her belly, and up. When he reached the underside of her breast, she smiled and covered his hand with hers to stop any more dangerous exploration.

"Mom? Did you want to talk about something, because if not—"

Her mother heaved a noisy sigh, wrought with emotion. "I didn't want to have to break the news to you this way, dear, but—"

"What news? Is there something wrong? Is Dad okay?"

"Dad's fine. He's out shopping for a new riding

mower today. The problem is, I had a doctor visit, and they found some lumps in my breast."

Her voice was quivery, on the verge of cracking, and Macy's heart lurched.

"Mom!" She sat up, tugging the sheet over her chest.

"Now don't get too upset. They did a biopsy, and they're not cancerous. They're just some kind of lumps. The doctor said I drink too much caffeine is all."

"But it's nothing to worry about, right? You're going to be okay?"

"I imagine so, but that's not the point. The point is, I had to have a biopsy and worry about having breast cancer all by myself, because you couldn't be bothered to check your messages."

"Mom, I'm sorry. I had no idea."

"And you know how your father is about health issues. He wouldn't talk about it at all. I had to suffer in silence all that time."

Macy leaned against a pillow and tried not to sound annoyed. "I'm really sorry."

This was such a typical episode of Thomaston family drama, Macy could have scripted it herself. If their life had been a commercial, this is where the product pitch would come in—the Thomaston Family, we're neurotic so you can feel better about your own life.

On the other end of the line, her mother was making sniffling sounds, which was a total buzz kill. Not even the sight of Griffin beside her could cheer Macy up now. She was suddenly seven years old again, miserably fat, eating Ho Hos and watching *Scooby Doo* while her mother sat on the couch in her green terry-cloth housecoat pouting about one thing or another.

"I joined a breast cancer support group," her mother said. "Those ladies have really helped me cope with my family's emotional distance during this ordeal."

"You joined a breast cancer support group? But I thought your lumps were benign."

"Does it really matter? What matters is that I thought I had breast cancer, and there was no one to support me through that horrible process."

Macy couldn't think of any sensible response. Maybe a support group was exactly what her mother needed. That is, until they found out she was a fraud and just using them to get sympathy. Or something. She wasn't quite sure what her mother needed, except perhaps some kind of mood-enhancing medication.

"Have you talked to the doctor about maybe getting a prescription for an antidepressant? Maybe that would help you feel better."

Her mother sobbed loudly into the phone, and Macy winced. Not the intended consequence, but then, she'd once witnessed her mom sobbing loudly over a rotten head of lettuce, so this should not have come as a surprise.

"You think I'm crazy now? Because I have a medical condition and sought out a support network to help me through it?"

"No, I don't think you're crazy." She cast a weary glance at Griffin, who offered a sympathetic wince in return. "I just think you might be feeling kind of down, and maybe some medication would help. That's all. It has nothing to do with your mental health."

"Don't you condescend to me!" her mother said, then hung up the phone.

Macy turned the phone off, then stared dumbly at it. Would it do any good to call back? Had she just been the catalyst that would send her mother into a deep depression? Was there any point in worrying?

"What was that all about? Is your mom okay?"

She slid down in bed and covered her face with the pillow, just as she'd thought about doing before the phone call. It had been a much more sensible plan than actually dialing her parents' phone number.

"She's fine," she said, her voice muffled by the pillow, which was cool and soft and smelled like dryer sheets.

"She's having some kind of health issue."

"More like some kind of craziness issue. She doesn't have breast cancer, but she's joined a breast cancer support group so she can be whiny and get lots of attention from people who actually need sympathy and attention."

"Wow."

"I'm pretty sure this is somehow my fault. Because I didn't answer my phone or check my messages, and because I'm basically an evil and selfish daughter."

"Doesn't she have friends or family close by who could be there for her in her, um…time of need?"

"She has five goldfish, no friends and her sisters all live far, far away from her where they won't have to listen to her whining. I think they didn't even give her their phone numbers. Smart women."

"I guess you get the crazy parent award," he said, lifting the pillow from her face and pulling her against him.

"Am I a tribute to the endurance of the human spirit or what?"

"Absolutely."

"I feel like I need to do something. If I don't make amends, she won't call me for six months, and then she'll spend another six months making me feel guilty for not getting in touch with her for six months. It's a no-win situation."

"Maybe you could go visit her."

"Oh, God. Shut your mouth."

"They're in Fresno, right? That's only a few hours' drive."

"Three hours. I thought we were going to spend this weekend in bed celebrating your promotion."

"You're not looking like you'll be much fun, anyway."

"Sure I will. Just give me some hard liquor, and I'll be a barrel of fun in fifteen minutes."

"I've got a better idea. We'll drive out to see your parents, and I can meet them."

Macy's heart lurched in her chest, and her stomach twisted into one of those complicated sailing knots.

"Um," she said, desperately trying to think of a way out of this mess.

But part of her loved that Griffin wanted to meet her parents. And another part of her had the common sense to remember that she'd entered into this relationship with him under a really crappy, dishonest pretense, and any sort of emotional bonding that took place now was only going to end in misery.

"You don't want me to meet your parents?"

"I'm a little surprised you'd want to meet them after what I've told you thus far."

Propped up on one elbow, he smiled at her. She couldn't get over how much she loved this side of him that wasn't competitive or cutthroat or even remotely obnoxious. He was a dream guy outside the office.

Which, in a way, totally and completely sucked.

She was anything but a dream girl, considering.

"I want to know everything about you. And your parents are part of who you are, so I want to know them, too."

"Please don't say things like that," she said, smiling. "If my parents are part of who I am, I'm in big trouble."

"Sometimes our parents shape us by being the thing we bounce off. They're like the mold we have to break out of, making us define ourselves by how we're different from them."

"Wow, that's pretty profound. I think I like your theory."

"So let's go. It'll make your mother happy."

"Or she may just get really pissed off that I dropped in unannounced with a visitor, therefore not giving her a chance to clean the house or prepare a meal or make herself look suitably miserable for the meeting."

"We'll call when we're twenty minutes out. How about that?"

Macy wanted to produce some logical reason not to do this, but then again, she didn't have the heart to tell Griffin no, not when he was being so sweet and when the trip really would likely placate her mother.

"Have I ever told you that you're a really cool guy?"

He smiled. "No, but this would be a good time to point it out."

"You, Griffin Reed, are a really cool guy, and I'm not just saying that because we're in bed together or because you're my soon-to-be boss."

"Thanks," he said.

"How about this—we'll go, but we won't stay long, okay? We get in and out, quick and relatively painless."

He leaned down and kissed her. It was a long, sweet kiss that felt more intimate than any other thing they'd done together. Intimate in a good way, and in a bad way. The kind of intimate that came with taking their relationship to the next level, even as Macy was dragging her feet and trying to keep them from going there.

14

GRIFFIN HADN'T DRIVEN on Highway 99 in years, and he'd forgotten how incredibly flat and vast the great central valley of California was. So different from San Francisco with its jammed-together buildings bursting at the seams with people and hills and cars and noise.

Beside him, Macy rode quietly in the passenger seat. She'd sunken into what he could only guess was a state of dread over the visit with her parents. His first instinct was to ask, hey, how bad could they really be, when they'd produced a woman like Macy? But then he remembered the whole feigned breast-cancer thing and realized maybe her sense of dread wasn't exactly misplaced.

Really, he was the one who should have been freaking out. And he was, sort of. He'd just volunteered to meet the parents.

And the more he thought about it, the more he felt as if he was flying a small aircraft while both enjoying the incredible freedom of soaring in the sky and seized by the terror that at any moment he could crash into the ground. He couldn't exactly sustain each of these emotions within himself at the same time, but rather he waffled between the two—one minute elated and the next terrified.

Why he wanted to meet Macy's parents all of a sudden, he couldn't say. He just knew it was time. He knew he was falling hard for Macy, and that he wanted to take their relationship to the next level.

Gone was his desire to have her just because she was beautiful, or just because she was a challenge. In the place of that desire were real, undeniable feelings for her. He couldn't help wonder now if he'd known subconsciously all along how right she could be for him, and that's what had led him to want her in the first place.

And yet, what if he was wrong? What if this was all a huge mistake? As of Monday, he'd be her boss, their work relationship would be seriously strained if their personal relationship didn't work out. And even if it did work out, would his girlfriend really want to have him as her superior?

Doubtful.

But they'd cross that bridge when they came to it. Knowing Macy's sense of ambition, which was equal to his, it was quite possible she'd want to move to a new ad agency soon enough, anyway.

All he knew was, he couldn't give up this thing with Macy now. It felt too good, too right—so much better than any other relationship he'd had. So much more full of potential.

"We're about twenty minutes out. Guess I should call my mom now," Macy said, sounding none too thrilled about the prospect.

"I could make the call if you want."

"No, you'll get to meet them soon enough. Last thing I need right now is my mother grilling you over the phone about whether we're practicing safe sex."

"Yikes. You really think she'd do that?"

"She gave my first boyfriend a box of condoms for Christmas."

"Wow."

"Yeah. She was a public health nurse before she retired to drive me insane."

"So is it too late for me to back out of this visit?"

She cast him the look of death.

"Joking!"

Macy dug her cell phone out of her purse and dialed.

"Hi, Mom," she said a moment later. "I've got a little surprise for you."

A pause.

"No, I'm not sending you and Dad on a cruise. I'm twenty minutes outside of Fresno with a friend, and we thought we'd stop in for a visit."

Another pause. Griffin could hear a high-pitched voice coming from the phone, like a tiny mouse talking.

"Yes, I realize that. That's why I'm calling ahead, so we're not just dropping in completely unexpectedly."

More mouse-talking.

"I just want to visit—that's all!" A pause. "Okay, bye."

She hung up the phone and tossed it back in her bag. Griffin glanced over and caught her looking utterly disgusted.

"We'll take the next exit," Macy said, and he merged into the right lane.

"So that didn't go so well?" he dared to ask.

"As well as expected. She's pissed that we're dropping in unannounced, and she wants us to know that she won't be making a fancy dinner—no meat loaf and pineapple upside-down cake on such short notice."

"Damn. No meat loaf."

Macy finally laughed.

Two miles later, they exited, and he followed Macy's directions through side roads and neighborhoods until they reached her parents' driveway. The house was a typical fifties ranch house, short on architectural detail and big on shrubbery.

Macy heaved a nervous sigh. Griffin reached over and placed his hand on top of hers.

"We'll get through this," he said, trying to look serious.

She laughed. "And if not, we can at least say we had Las Vegas."

They got out of the car, walked up a cracking sidewalk, and Griffin wondered one more time what the hell he was doing. But he also was incredibly curious to meet Macy's parents, to see her childhood home, to get to know the life that had shaped her into the woman he was falling in love with.

Crazy, but true.

Macy rang the doorbell, then tried the doorknob without waiting for someone to answer. It was unlocked, and she pushed the door open. "Hello?" she called into the house.

A woman with a pretty round face and wide hips appeared in the hallway. She had curly blond hair and Macy's soft brown eyes. She wore a faded green T-shirt tucked into circa 1990 stonewashed jeans, and when she looked at Griffin, she plastered on a big smile.

"You must be Macy's friend."

"Mom, this is Griffin Reed. Griffin, this is my mom, Joy Thomaston."

She shook his hand, then embraced Macy in a half-hearted hug.

"It's good to see you both, but I don't understand what this unplanned visit is all about. I'm not dying or anything."

"I know, Mom. Your call just reminded me that I haven't come to visit in a while, and I thought it would be nice to see you. I felt bad about the way our call ended."

"You know there won't be much of an inheritance when I die," her mother said, crossing her arms over her ample chest.

"What does that have to do with anything? And why should I even care?"

Mrs. Thomaston sighed heavily. She wasn't going to win any acting awards, but Griffin could tell by Macy's stiff posture that her mother was already getting to her.

"I may not have cancer now, but all these lumps will certainly make it harder for me to tell if I do have malignant ones growing. I know that's on your mind, and I know you're probably here hoping you can benefit somehow from my illness."

Macy's tolerant expression vanished, to be replaced by pure outrage. "We're leaving," she said, her calm voice edged with fury.

She turned toward the door, but Griffin caught her hand in his. "Wait," he said. "I'm sure your mom didn't mean that the way it sounded."

He was lying, but he didn't see any reason to let their relationship crumble in his presence.

"I'm sure you're just under a lot of stress because of your health issues—right, Mrs. Thomaston?" he said.

She looked confused, but then she gave in. "You have no idea how much."

"We drove all this way. There's no sense in leaving before we've even gotten to visit," he said to Macy, and she cast him a death glare again, but she yielded to his tugging on her hand, and a minute later they were sitting in the family room, which looked as though it had last been redecorated some time in the eighties.

Peach leather sofas, mint-green speckled carpeting, lots of pastel-colored abstract paintings and a TV dominated the room.

"Can I get you two something to drink? We're all out of sodas, and I only have decaf coffee."

"I'll have a coffee," Macy said.

"Me, too."

As soon as her mom was gone from the room, she mouthed the words "Let's go."

Griffin shook his head. "No way. We're staying."

"What's the matter with you? Are you a masochist?"

He shrugged and whispered. "Your mom seems nice, maybe just a little…"

"Insane?"

"I didn't say that."

"You didn't have to."

"Are those pictures of you?" he said, nodding to some brass-framed photos on the bookcase across the room.

"Oh, God. No, those are my evil twin's photos."

"You've already told me you don't have any siblings, remember?" he said as he got up and went to the photos.

"Oh, right," she said, following him. "I need to remember to lie more often."

On the shelves sat a photographic history of Macy's life, from her sweet chubby-cheeked baby photos to her gawky preteen years, from her toothless elementary school grins to her plump senior portrait. She looked like a different person altogether now, but the one constant was her eyes. Wide and brown and full of warmth, they never changed throughout her many different phases.

"You were a cute kid," he said.

"I was a total geek."

"We all were."

"You weren't. You were Mr. All-Star American Jock. You were the kind of guy who never would have noticed me in school."

He draped an arm over her shoulder and pulled her closer. "That's not true."

"Please. I once had a crush on a guy just like you, all through high school. Once, I got up the nerve to talk to him in the hallway...."

"And what happened?"

"I walked up and said, 'Hi, I'm Macy, from your chemistry class,' and he said, 'Huh? You're not in my class.' But I was. I sat three seats behind him the entire year, and he never once noticed me."

"He was an asshole then."

"True. But does that mean you're claiming you were always such a nice guy, you would have noticed me even when I was fat?"

"Absolutely." But he was lying. He probably wouldn't have, he realized, and it made him see just how much people could miss out on by not looking past the surface, by always judging outward appearances.

"Coffee's almost ready," Mrs. Thomaston called from the kitchen. "Who wants milk and sugar?"

"I'll take milk, but no sugar," Macy called back.

"Same here," Griffin said.

"Watch, she'll load down both our cups with so much sugar you'll think you're drinking melted coffee ice cream. She does it every time."

"Why?"

"Because that's the way *she* likes it."

"Then why did she even ask what we wanted?"

"Beats me. Some kind of weird control thing."

They sat down, and a minute later Mrs. Thomaston carried in a tray of coffee cups and sat it on the glass table in front of the sofa.

"Where's Dad?" Macy asked.

"He should be home any time now. He's been out all day shopping for a riding mower."

Griffin sipped his coffee and nearly gagged on the

sweetness of it. He set the cup aside and listened as Macy's mother talked about lawn problems and unreliable landscaping services.

Macy took a few sips and set her cup aside as well.

Griffin felt a crazy urge to protect her from her mother, at the same time that he wanted to know everything about her family life. He felt as if he was learning about layers of her personality he hadn't even mined yet, layers he hadn't realized were there until today.

Macy as a carefree little girl, Macy as an insecure teenager, Macy as a daughter to a mother who hadn't wanted to have more kids because one was more than she could handle.

And now, Macy as the woman he loved.

He loved her.

Somewhere between San Francisco and Fresno, somewhere between the crowded city and the vast suburbs, it had become an indisputable fact in his head.

Which meant he had to tell her, when the time was right. Whether she was ready to hear it or not.

MACY WANTED to run for her life. Griffin could stay, but she felt claustrophobic, as though if she didn't get out of her parents' house now, it would suck all the breath out of her.

But she knew running wasn't going to do her any good. Her mother would find her one way or another.

And this was her life, anyway. She had to face it. There weren't any wealthy missing parents searching for her, there weren't any get-out-of-this-family-free cards. Her parents were a part of who she was, and if she didn't come to terms with that, her mother would always have the power to drive her crazy.

It felt good to have Griffin there beside her. She made a mental note to thank him later—if they survived this visit—for forcing her to come here and face the problem of her mother head-on.

Her mother had stopped talking about the lawn at some point and was now asking Griffin questions.

"How did you two meet?" she was asking.

"We work together," Griffin said.

"And you're a couple?"

He put his arm around Macy. "Absolutely."

Whoa, there. Is that what they were calling it now? When had this happened? Macy blinked, and blinked again. Somehow this office affair had gotten completely out of control, and she was beyond stupid for not noticing it. She and Griffin were now a...couple?

Holy crap.

"Are you planning to get married? Is that why you're here? To announce your engagement?" her mother said, eyeing Macy's naked ring finger.

Leave it to her to take the conversation from vaguely uncomfortable to totally freaking awkward in a matter of minutes.

"Um, we're not quite at that stage," Griffin said diplomatically. "But I'm absolutely crazy about Macy."

"You know she's not had a lot of experience at relationships," her mother said. "She was quite the late bloomer."

Griffin clearly didn't know how to respond to that

one. Macy figured it was best not to point out that she'd actually had plenty of experiences as an adult—none of which she'd chosen to share with her family.

Her mother nodded at the chubby photos across the room. "She had a weight problem all through her childhood years. Cleared up as soon as she moved away from home. I figured it was bulimia or maybe anorexia, but I never could get her to seek help."

Griffin was still speechless. Macy, having heard it all before, had nothing else to say.

"Have you seen her purging…or eating like a bird?"

"I'm sure Macy doesn't have any eating disorder. I've never seen her act anything but completely normal about food."

Same arguments Macy had used until she was blue in the face. Eventually, she had to accept the fact that the reality her mother built in her head was the only one she was capable of believing. In all the years Macy had lived in San Francisco, her mother had never visited her there because she believed the city was full of drugged-out hippies and militant homosexuals. Didn't matter whether it was true or not—that's what she believed and there was no changing her mind.

As it was with everything.

And then came the inevitable. "I hope you two are practicing safe sex."

Griffin nudged Macy's foot with his, and she did her best to keep a straight face.

"Absolutely," he said without hesitation.

"You realize there is a failure rate with condoms, and

that you're not protected from disease during oral sex. Have you been tested since your last sexual partners?"

"Tested and clean, I can assure you."

He was holding up exceptionally well. Macy wouldn't have blamed him if he'd run screaming from the house.

But he didn't, and she realized that meant something to her. She'd introduced a few guys to her family, but he was the first guy she could see tolerating additional family get-togethers.

Which, sadly, wasn't going to happen.

They survived another hour with her mother, until her father arrived home. Thankfully, Frank Thomaston had enough sense not to talk to his grown daughter's male friends about birth control, but he mostly didn't talk at all. His idea of a good dinner conversation consisted mainly of "Pass the butter," and "Thank you."

They sat on the sofa watching ESPN with him for a while—long enough that getting up to leave wouldn't seem rude—and then they tried to leave. But when they peeked into the kitchen to say goodbye to Joy, she had her hands buried in a glob of ground beef.

"You can't leave now," she said. "I'm making meat loaf!"

"But, you said you weren't cooking, and we still have to get back to the city tonight."

Macy glanced up at the kitchen clock, shaped like a head of lettuce. Which for the first time struck her as bizarrely appropriate given the historic rotten-lettuce incident. It was almost four.

"I changed my mind. I thought it would be nice to

have a family dinner together for a change, since your friend is here."

Which meant she liked Griffin. Really liked him.

Macy wasn't sure whether to be pleased or disturbed by that. But it didn't really matter. She wasn't kidding herself about the nature of their relationship, and no matter how much they might be enjoying each other's company outside the office, there was still the fact that Griffin had very few of the qualities of her dream guy.

Arrogant, overconfident jock did not equal keeper material in her book. He was the kind of guy she'd spent her adult life avoiding. The only reason they were getting along was because they had great sexual chemistry.

That was it. Period. End of story.

She eyed Griffin, and he shrugged. "I don't know, Mom. This would put us getting back into the city late."

"Oh, stop it. You'll have to eat sooner or later, anyway, and dinner will be done in twenty minutes. You can spare twenty minutes, can't you?"

"Wow, that's pretty fast for a meat loaf, isn't it?" Macy said.

"I'm making it in the microwave."

"Oh." Yum.

"Sit down," her mother said. "There are playing cards in the basket in the middle of the table. You can play rummy."

Major flashback. Macy hadn't played rummy since her miserable sophomore year in high school when everyone else was starting to date, and she was stuck home with her parents and a deck of cards. Sometimes she'd even been pitiful enough to play solitaire while pretending her imaginary boyfriend was sitting across the table from her. Maybe watching her lovingly, being astounded by her card-playing abilities, complimenting her when she made an especially impressive move.

"Rummy," Macy said, making a face at Griffin. "Yay."

He pulled out a chair and sat down, grabbed the deck of cards, did a lightning-fast shuffle and dealt a hand to each of them.

Macy reluctantly sat down across from him and picked up her hand.

"You'll have to refresh me on the rules," he said, smiling at her as if he was perfectly happy to be there at her mother's Formica table, sitting in her pink-cushioned rolling chairs.

Her teenage fantasy come to life. Dear God. How had this happened?

He was cuter than any of the guys she'd spent those years pining after, and smarter, but he was most certainly one of them. He probably still had the letterman jackets in his closet to prove it.

The uneasy feeling in Macy's belly grew to hurricane proportions, and she couldn't remember the rules for rummy.

"I've forgotten," she said. "Mom, can you refresh us?"

Her mother filled them in, but Macy couldn't focus.

She'd spent her whole adult life trying to distance herself from the kind of person she'd been as a teenager, and that included pining after guys like Griffin. And now here she sat with one she not only liked, but feared she was falling for.

She stared dumbly at the hand Griffin had dealt her. And then her mother's instructions began to sink into her brain. Really, the rules had been there all along, buried in her memory from countless nights spent at home with her parents.

And being here now with Griffin? It was just a case of old habits being hard to break. There had been no revenge of the nerd, because the nerd had seen her chance with the office jock and thrown herself at him as if he was a life-sized brownie sundae.

15

GRIFFIN GLANCED OVER at Macy sitting in the passenger seat. She'd been a little morose all afternoon at her parents' place, and nothing he'd tried had broken her out of the funk.

"You want to talk about it?" he asked.

"Hmm?" She looked at him as if he'd just startled her out of a daze.

"Your dark mood—do you want to talk about it?"

"Oh, sorry. I guess I just get this way around my parents."

"Are you sure they're all that's bothering you? I mean, they're not here now, but your mood still is."

She stared out the passenger window, not answering for a while.

"I used to be such a nerd growing up, I didn't have a life, so I spent all my time fantasizing about the one I would have someday. I'd be pretty, have a glamorous job… I'd be confident, a risk-taker, the kind of woman people write books and TV shows about."

"Sounds like you've accomplished all your goals in spades then."

More silence, and then, "I guess."

"So what's wrong?"

"I never could figure out how to exorcize the miserable fat kid. She's still here. She's just dressed up in cool kids' clothing."

Griffin tried not to laugh. He really tried. But he failed. "Why would you even want to? I mean, you are who you are, and I think you're amazing just like you are."

"Maybe I imagined, I dunno, that the confidence part would be easier. That I'd always know the right thing to do, and I'd never have any huge problems to deal with."

"That was just adolescent idealism. You know better now. But as far as confidence goes, you have no reason not to be sure of yourself. You're amazing at everything you do."

"Not always. Sometimes I do stupid things."

"Like what?"

She glanced over at him, but in the waning light, her face was shadowed and he couldn't quite read the expression in her eyes.

"Like have an affair with a guy in my office that I know will be doomed and that will likely complicate our lives unnecessarily."

"Complication can be a good thing."

"But seriously. We keep saying, 'after this weekend we're done,' or 'just one more night and we're done,' and now look at us. You've met my parents, for God's sake."

"So?"

"So now I'm going to spend the next three years fielding questions from my mother about what ever happened to that nice boy Gavin."

"Gavin?"

"She'll forget your name by next Tuesday."

Outside the car, the rural scenery of Gilroy rolled past, and the scent of garlic filled the air from the many garlic farms surrounding the town. This was a much more enjoyable part of the drive than going north on 99, but the sometimes windy, narrow road meant he had to pay close attention to the wheel.

"I liked your parents," he said. "They were nice."

Also a little wacky, and clearly not aware of what a great daughter they had, but that was their own loss.

"Yeah, well. I liked having you there. I mean, I'm sorry you had to eat microwaved meat loaf, but as far as parental visits go, that was one of the more pleasant ones. Having you there helped."

"So I'm still not seeing what the big problem is."

"I'm not supposed to like you!" she said a little too vehemently.

"You're not?"

"I'm supposed to be cool and detached, because this is our little meaningless office fling, and instead I'm falling for you."

"Oh."

"That's what's wrong!"

Griffin was tempted to point out that he was falling crazy in love with her, but in her current state, he wasn't sure how the news would be taken. Better to wait until she was in a cheerier mood.

"You know, it's not unheard of for office romances to work out," he offered, searching for solid ground.

She sighed. "I'm supposed to fall in love with a

dark, brooding lone-wolf type. I'm not supposed to be with a gregarious all-star jock."

"Did you visit a fortune teller?"

"I just know. We all have our fantasy mate, and…"

"And I remind you too much of those guys in high school who ignored you and made fun of you?"

She said nothing.

He wanted to tell her to get over it, but he realized that would make him sound like an insensitive jerk, and probably dark, brooding lone wolves never said insensitive things to their lovers. He also considered pointing out that maybe she'd taken all those romance novels she read too seriously, but again, it wasn't going to score him any points.

"Macy, I know we're both ad people. We deal with images all the time. But this is a case where you have to move beyond the image. You're putting the wrong spin on this situation."

Finally, she smiled. "You mean, I should be looking for the value-added features in our relationship?"

"Absolutely. Spin it the right way, and you can sell yourself anything."

"I like that."

They rode a few minutes longer in silence as they neared the entrance to Highway 101.

And when he was about to take the on-ramp, Macy said, "Ooh, look. McDonald's drive-through. Let's get milkshakes."

Griffin slowed the car and flipped on the turn signal. He wasn't positive he'd completely dodged the our-relationship-is-doomed bullet, but once he had Macy home, naked and thoroughly satisfied, he was pretty damn sure he could sell her anything. Including a commitment with him.

In fact, after getting to know Macy privately from all these different angles, falling for her harder and harder, he was beginning to understand that he wouldn't have any peace in his life until he knew Macy was not only his for the night, but his for keeps.

MACY HAD SUGGESTED they go to his place tonight to avoid anymore phone calls from her mother, and Griffin was happy to oblige. He liked showing off his bachelor pad. It wasn't very big, but he'd done some remodeling, and he thought he'd done a damn good job.

Granite countertops, custom maple cabinets, refinished hardwood floors. He'd even painted the walls. Okay, they were all beige because he didn't know what other color would match everything, but still. It looked better than white.

Griffin had a feeling that this was his last chance to prove to Macy that he cared for her enough that their working together didn't matter. All that mattered was the way he felt, and of course, he realized, that wasn't exactly fair. The way she felt mattered just as much, and she'd already made clear her desire not to get themselves entangled any further.

He watched her checking out the books on his shelves as he undressed. She could browse all she wanted, but he had one thing in mind tonight. Sexual persuasion.

His shelves contained lots of American classics like

Hemingway, Thoreau and Emerson, and a hodgepodge of more contemporary classics. He'd studied English in college and had first started collecting classics to impress anyone who checked out his bookshelves, but once he'd finished school and had time to read for pleasure, he'd discovered that he actually liked the classics.

"Have you read all these?" she asked.

"Yep, most of them a couple of times."

"I never would have labeled you a literary type."

"It's my dirty little secret. I might lose my all-star jock image if word ever got out."

"Your only dirty secret?" she asked, eyeing him with mock suspicion.

"Well, that and the fact that I'm about to sleep with one of my subordinates."

"Oh, so now that you've got me alone in your apartment, I'm your subordinate."

"Only if it turns you on," he said, catching her hand in his and pulling her close so that she could not just see the evidence of his arousal, but feel it, too.

Her body molded against his, and she rested her head on his chest instead of looking up at him. The gesture created a heavy feeling in his gut, as if he was about to lose something dear.

"No comment," she whispered.

"Do you ever read anything besides romance novels?" he asked.

"Why? You have a problem with them?"

"Not at all. I'm all for guys in billowy shirts and girls in revealing dresses."

"Haven't you ever heard that saying about not judging a book by its cover?"

"Sure. I was just wondering if you've ever read Hemingway's *A Farewell to Arms.*"

"I did in college. I remember it was really depressing. I hate tragic love stories."

"I feel the same way right now that I did when I read that book—like a world has ended."

She frowned. "Why?"

"I don't want to just gaze across the room at you knowing I can't have you. What's the fun of that?"

"You've got me right now."

"I mean tomorrow, and next month, and next year."

She was silent for a moment, a little crease forming between her eyebrows.

"Sometimes it's more fun to want something than to have it."

"In your case, I can confirm that's definitely not true."

"Well, thanks, but—"

"I know, I know. I've heard it all before." Griffin's throat tightened. He'd never felt as if so much was at stake. He'd never felt so wildly, blindly in love before, and he needed to know that Macy shared his intense feelings. He tilted her chin up until she was looking him in the eyes.

"I love you," he said, and the words felt as natural and simple as the act of breathing.

Macy's expression transformed then, but not in the way he was expecting. He watched all the softness vanish from her features, replaced by a hardness that he knew had to spell bad news.

"Griffin, there's something I have to tell you," she said.

He imagined the possibilities. Maybe she had huge, unbelievable credit card debt, or maybe she had a weird foot fetish, or maybe she was a member of a cult. He could get past that stuff.

"Don't look so solemn," he said, nudging her. "How bad could it be?"

"I've got something really awful to tell you." She broke free from his grasp and paced across the room, putting some distance between them, leaving him standing there naked and exposed.

"What?"

"I had an agenda last weekend when we went to Las Vegas. I was trying to dumb you down with sex."

"What?" His brain tried to process her words, but she wasn't making any sense.

"Didn't you feel kind of fuzzy-headed Monday after our trip, when you were doing the presentation?"

Griffin recalled how he'd felt as if his thoughts were stuck in molasses. His brain had been operating at reduced capacity that day and even the next day. But no way was it because of sex…was it?

"Yeah, so?" he said.

Macy looked as if she was about to confess to capital murder. "A friend of mine is a scientist, and she'd just completed a study on the effects of sex on human intelligence. She told me about how she'd discovered that sex temporarily reduces our mental capacity, and—"

"That's impossible." Griffin crossed his arms and paced across the room. When he spotted his pants and boxers on the floor, he grabbed them and tugged them on, his mind stumbling around the facts.

Stumbling. Was it really impossible? He'd had sex earlier today. It's possible he wasn't thinking at full capacity.

Damn it.

"Griffin, I'm sorry. I feel awful about having manipulated you. It was a nasty, underhanded thing to do." Macy was walking toward him now, but he didn't want her too near, where he could forget what he was supposed to be pissed off about.

He took a step back away from her. "What do you mean you manipulated me?"

She sighed, and her pained expression grew even darker. "I didn't come at all during that weekend in Vegas."

Whoa! He stopped his pacing, and the air left his lungs.

"You really were faking it? The entire time?"

She nodded. "It was an act," she said, her gaze focused on the shiny wood floors.

"But why?" Though the truth was lurking in the dark recesses of his brain, trying to find its way out.

"I wanted to keep you from being mentally sharp during the presentation."

"That's...diabolical." Big word for a guy who'd just been dumbed down by sex, but he couldn't think of a better way to describe it.

"If it's any consolation, it was really hard not to come with you. I definitely got the bad end of the deal."

"It's not any consolation, not when I thought we were two adults being upfront with each other." He grabbed his shirt and tugged it over his head, shoved his feet into his shoes and headed for the door.

But damn it, this was his apartment. She was the one who needed to get the hell out.

The more he thought about what she'd done, the more pissed off he got. His thoughts were emerging from the molasses, and now he understood exactly what was going on here. He'd been had.

Macy came toward him again, but he held up a hand to stop her.

"I'm very, very sorry," she said. "It was a crappy thing to do."

"You need to leave now," he said as he opened the door. "I'll call you a cab. You can wait in the lobby of the building until it comes."

She made a weird gasping sound, and he realized she was crying. She picked up her purse from the coffee table, then cast a pitiful look in his direction. He almost wanted to take her in his arms, but how could he?

When would he know when she was being fake and when she was being real? Had he fallen in love with a real woman, or an act?

"Could we please talk about this first?" she said. "It's more complicated than it sounds."

"We're finished talking. I don't know when you're lying and when you're telling the truth, anyway." Macy wasn't the woman he thought he'd fallen in love with at all.

He'd fallen for her act. Like a fool.

He could fall once, but not twice. "If you want the damn promotion so badly," he said, "You can have it."

16

MACY FELT like a small, slimy toad. She'd known telling Griffin the truth would suck, but she hadn't anticipated just how awful she'd feel once he knew about her betrayal.

She'd taken a cab home, then tried for hours to sleep, but whenever she dozed off, she was awakened by nightmares. She got up early Sunday morning and tossed the sheet back on the bed, which mocked her with its emptiness now.

Where she and Griffin had made love less than a day ago, she'd now get to while away her days and nights alone, left with nothing but cold memories of a relationship she'd let herself get too invested in. A relationship that had been doomed from the start.

She spent the morning cleaning the apartment with her old Guns N' Roses CDs turned up extra loud in the hope that the screeching heavy metal would drown out her thoughts. It only occasionally worked.

Sometime around noon, Carson had called, telling her another trip to Vegas had come up for tomorrow, and would she like to come since it involved the art side of the project? While her stomach had lurched at the thought of going back to work, she'd jumped at the chance to get the hell away from the office.

He said Griffin wouldn't need to make this trip, and panic swirled in her belly. What if he was planning to quit because of her? She wouldn't be able to live with herself.

Once Macy had cleaned the apartment within an inch of its life, she went to the bathroom and took a shower, lingering too long under the hot water. Then she dressed in a pair of black yoga pants and a stretchy white tank top, pulled her wet hair back into a ponytail, and went to the kitchen to look for chocolate.

All she found were some old, grayish-looking chocolate chips in the refrigerator, a box of See's Candies left over from Christmas with only the hated pieces of toffee left in the box and a disgusting chocolate-flavored energy bar purchased over a year ago during one of her misguided healthy-eating campaigns.

"Damn it," she muttered.

She wished like crazy she hadn't estranged herself from her best friend. Sure, she had other friends, but she'd always turned to Lauren when she needed a shoulder to cry on or a chocolate delivery person.

And really, if her love life and her work life were going to be royally screwed, she needed to fix something. She needed to make amends with Lauren.

But the thought of doing so left her wanting chocolate even more. She went to the fridge and pulled out the bag of chocolate chips, made a point not to look at the best-if-used-by date on the package, and flopped down on the couch.

Fifteen minutes later, the bag was empty, and she'd worked up the nerve to pick up the phone.

She grabbed the receiver from the end table and dialed Lauren's number. As the phone rang, her stomach churned. After four rings, the answering machine picked up, and Macy debated whether to hang up or leave a message. She'd just hang up, except Lauren almost always screened her calls.

Then she heard the beep. "Lauren, it's me, Macy. Please pick up the phone if you're there. I owe you an apology, and we need to talk. Lauren? Please? I know you're there reading the paper—"

"Talk," Lauren said, her voice on the line now.

"I'm sorry. Can we be friends again? I need a friend right now."

Lauren made an offended noise. "So this call is all about you needing a friend right now? It had nothing to do with me needing a friend to stand by me when I'm trying to ward off attention from a guy I don't want? It has nothing to do with me needing a friend not to give out my phone number to said guy?"

"I'm so sorry. I was a lousy friend. I should have been on your side and not Carson's." Macy peered into the yellow chocolate chip bag, hoping she'd overlooked a few.

"Give me one good reason why I should forgive you?"

"I'll pay to have your number changed?"

"I don't want to have my number changed. I want Carson to stop calling me."

"I'll talk to him and make sure there are no more calls. I just thought—"

"I know, I know, you just thought I need to get hooked up with some guy so I can get married and become a breeder and live happily ever after."

"That's not it. I just thought you two were good together."

"Spare me the fairy-tale endings, okay? I'm happy alone, and that's the way I want it. If we're going to be friends, you have to accept that."

"I promise, no more meddling in your love life." Though Macy really didn't get it. While she was always looking for the right guy and never finding him, Lauren was so uninterested in guys, they couldn't help but be interested in her. Macy needed to learn from that disinterested aloofness.

But no, she'd tried before, and she'd failed. She couldn't hide the fact that she loved men, loved being in love, and wanted to find a guy who would love her.

The thought nearly made her lose her chocolate chips. She'd found that guy and she'd screwed him royally. She had no one to blame for her unhappiness but herself. She'd gotten so caught up in stupid images, she'd never stopped to consider the true nature of their relationship.

"So what happened that's brought you groveling back to me?" Lauren asked, her tone less hostile now.

"I ruined everything with Griffin…. I told him about my efforts to dumb him down with sex, right after he told me he loved me."

"Oh, dear God. Why do you have to be so honest?"

"He was furious. I think he might turn down the promotion now just so he'll never have to work with me again. Or maybe not. I'm not sure."

"Turn it down for you?"

"Because of me." Macy filled Lauren in on all the details of the past week. When she finished, Lauren was silent.

"Are you that shocked by my failure?"

"No, I'm just…well, I'm sorry. I gave you bad advice."

"You have nothing to be sorry for. You were just trying to help me get the promotion, and you couldn't have known Griffin would fall in love with me."

Her throat tightened up at those last words, and tears stung her eyes. She'd never minded playing games casually—playing the clueless ingenue, letting guys believe whatever they wanted about her if it meant having the upper hand.

Until now. She'd never played with such high stakes before, and she'd never once wanted to stomp on any guy's emotions. Especially not Griffin's. Not after she'd gotten to know him.

"But in a way this is good news, right? Because if he doesn't want the promotion, that means you can take it."

Macy sighed. She'd tried to imagine that as a bright side, but it didn't work that way. "I've already told the senior partners I didn't want the job. I couldn't take the promotion now if it's offered to me. I'd always know I got it using underhanded means—and that I'd gotten it by stepping on other people. I couldn't live with that."

She'd been a little late remembering her principles, but better late than never.

"So what are you going to do?"

"I don't know. Quit my job and join the Peace Corps?"

"That's your grief talking. You'd be awful in a Third World country. You'd never get to wear cute suits or high heels, and there'd be no place to get your highlights done, no place to do a proper pedicure—"

"Okay, okay, I'm not Peace Corps material. But seriously, I'm not sure I can show my face in the same office as Griffin again."

"I think it'll do you good to face him and see that life will go on."

"What if he tells people what I did?"

"Then you might want to quit and join the Peace Corps."

"Very funny."

"Griffin seems like a guy with some principles—"

"Unlike me."

"I doubt he'd kiss and tell."

Lauren was probably right. Macy couldn't imagine Griffin sinking to her level. Even when he'd used his sex appeal to get ahead, he'd always done it in a harmless way. He'd never hurt anyone. Unlike Macy.

"This sucks."

Lauren was silent.

"What?" Macy finally said. "What are you thinking?"

"Oh, nothing. Just that if Griffin turns down the promotion, and you can't have it, maybe Carson will get it."

"Why do you care if he gets it or not?"

"I don't. It was just an idea that popped into my head, that's all."

Macy felt like an idiot for never having considered the possibility before. She'd been so focused on beating Griffin, she'd failed to look around at the competition. And Carson, always so laid back and casual, had never struck her as competition. But he'd be perfect for the job. Everyone loved him, and he'd never sleep with someone just to diminish their abilities.

"You know," she said. "I hope you're right. If Griffin doesn't want the job, I hope it's offered to Carson."

"There will be a million other opportunities for you," Lauren said.

"Thanks, I need all the confidence I can get right now."

"You sound like what you really need is a badly translated kung fu movie and a double pepperoni pizza."

"Would that be hoping for too much?"

"I'll be there in an hour."

"I'll call for pizza at the place on the corner if you'll pick it up."

Macy hung up the phone and forced herself to smile. Yes, an actual smile, because she'd read somewhere that the simple act of smiling could lead to happiness. She was willing to try anything at this point.

As she waited for Lauren to arrive, Macy read her e-mail—mostly junk—checked her cell-phone messages—three from her mother, two saying that she hoped to see that nice boy Garrett again soon—and rearranged all the CDs on her CD rack by alphabet and music genre.

When Lauren arrived with pizza, Macy realized she did have one little thing to feel good about. She might have lost a great guy, but at least she'd gotten back her best friend. And now if she could just find a reason to respect herself, she'd be well on her way to not feeling like crap.

Had she really thought she could blame her stupid decisions on a city? Even if it was Sin City? Had she actually gotten so desperate that she'd mistaken such a crazy notion for logic? For clear thinking?

Yes. She had.

They put in the movie and settled on the couch with cold cans of Coke and the box of pizza.

She took a piece out and bit into it. It tasted incredible, but it didn't make her feel any better.

"You think you are a talented pugilist?" the hot shirtless guy on the TV screen said. "You will feel my wrath."

Lauren snickered. "How many times do you think they can use the word *pugilist* in this movie?"

"I think they've already broken a world record."

She watched as the hot guy used a wooden pole to fight with the old guy who was missing two of his front teeth. What the old guy lacked in strength, he made up for in speed, and the match was pretty even. Of course, this was the world of martial arts films, where the usual logic of fighting didn't apply.

Macy tried to get lost in the laughable subtitles. But her mind kept wandering back to that simple yet oh, so diabolical phrase—What happens in Vegas stays in Vegas.

She'd never imagined how untrue it would be.

GRIFFIN STARED OUT at the bay, where the afternoon fog was just starting to roll in. A hard run across the Golden Gate Bridge and back hadn't cured him of his restlessness, and neither had another two miles along the beach.

The scents of eucalyptus and sea water were heavy in the air, and the cold dampness left him feeling as if he was running in an icy soup.

When he finally realized that it didn't matter how far he ran, he wasn't going to escape any of the demons lurking in his head, he stopped, walked along Crissy Field as he caught his breath and finally let his brain work over the problems. There was no avoiding them.

It didn't take long for him to realize how much he wanted to get a fresh start. He wasn't sure why he'd been putting it off for so many years, but maybe this mess with Macy was the impetus he needed to strike out on his own, leave Bronson and Wade, and start his own agency.

Clearly, Macy wanted the promotion more than he did or she never would have gone to such ends to increase her chances of getting it. So, with him out of the picture, she could have what she wanted, even if she didn't particularly deserve it after recent events.

What he wanted was the issue here. And as soon as the idea was fully formed in his head, he felt a surge of relief so huge, he wanted to jump up in the air and kick his heels together.

He'd do it. He'd turn down the promotion, put in his resignation tomorrow and move forward. He had enough in his emergency savings account to last him at least five months before he'd start running low on cash. That was enough time to get a business going, he hoped. It would have to be.

When he reached the car, he got in and grabbed his cell phone out of the passenger seat, then dialed Carson's number.

"Hey, man," he said when Carson answered. "It's me. Looks like the creative director job is still open."

"What are you talking about?"

Griffin filled him in on his decision.

"Whoa. You sure about this? You can't just drop your career because of some woman trouble."

"It's not her. She's just the one who made me realize what I really want to do. I know it sounds crazy, but hey."

"Sometimes the crazy ideas turn out to be the smartest ones in the end."

"Don't suppose you'd want to be hired away from your current job?"

Carson laughed. "Dude, I like you too much to go into business with you, know what I mean?"

"Yeah, I do. Thought I'd ask, anyway. I know a good ad man when I see one."

"I wonder how Macy's going to react to your leaving."

"She's a big girl. She can handle it, but if you could keep word of my departure to yourself for a while, that would be great. I want to break the news to the senior partners before anyone else hears."

"No problem. What's the deal with Macy, though? Aren't you two on speaking terms?"

"We were until last night when we parted ways for good."

"I still don't get that you two can't get along. You're clearly perfect for each other."

"It's complicated."

"Women always are."

True, but it felt wrong lumping Macy into the general category of all the women he'd dated. She stood away from the rest, maybe because of her deception, maybe because of the craziness of their relationship or maybe just because she was Macy.

Something was nagging at the back of his conscience, and he was struck with the feeling that he had to get off the phone and figure out what it was.

"Hey, I'd better go," he said.

"No problem. If you need to talk, you can reach me on my cell tomorrow and Tuesday."

"Oh, right, the meeting in Vegas with the photographer for the print ads."

"Yep, and the hotel's comping our trip again. I'll be living it up on their dime."

"Just be careful—if you happen to hook up with anyone while you're there, I hear sex is bad for your IQ."

Carson laughed. "What the hell are you talking about?"

Maybe it was better to just let him figure it out on his own. "Oh, nothing. It's just some dumb-ass study I heard about recently. It was probably funded by Celibates of America or something."

"Whatever, dude. You get some rest. I think the stress is going to your head."

When Griffin hung up the phone, his thoughts turned to that nagging sensation again.

Macy.

Not like the others.

Not like any other woman he'd ever known.

How many women would try to sex a man out of his intelligence, all for the sake of a job promotion?

He should have been pissed off about it, but she did tell him the truth, and honestly, she'd only played the game he'd started.

Sure, he'd used the sexual tension between them as a weapon at times. He'd occasionally tried to woo her with their attraction to each other all for the sake of winning in the office.

He was a competitor, and now he realized he'd been playing anything but honorably. So all she'd really done was sink to his level, and he couldn't blame her for that. At least she had the grace to feel guilty about her actions, come clean and apologize, whereas he hadn't even acknowledged until now that he'd been playing dirty at all.

He was the one who owed her an apology. And he was ashamed of himself now for letting himself get so fixated on winning the game that he'd forgotten to play fairly. Hell, if he'd learned about the sex study before Macy, he'd have done the same thing she did. No doubt.

He smiled. Then he laughed. Sex had a dumbing-down effect on the human animal.

He was living proof of that very fact.

17

MACY LOOKED OUT over the city, breathed in the hot, dry air and hugged herself. Here she was, back in Las Vegas, in a suite nearly identical to the one she'd stayed in the weekend before.

Here she was in the place where she'd tried to cast off all her inhibitions but had just ended up making a horrible mess instead. The memories of that wicked weekend left Macy with an achy, hollow feeling in her belly that refused to go away.

She'd spent all afternoon dealing with Golden Gate business, and all evening sitting in her room eating room service, watching crappy movies and feeling hopelessly sorry for herself.

She took in the sight of all the twinkling neon lights, then looked up at the night sky, where the stars were barely visible thanks to the ambient light from the city. What was she doing here? By herself. Again. It was too bad God wouldn't spell out all the answers for her in star patterns.

Down below, the sounds of nighttime in the city created a cacophony that made her feel like a lonely loser. While the rest of the city was partying, she was in her room alone.

Alone. Was that really such a bad thing? Weren't women of her age and generation supposed to relish being free and single?

Apparently so. Macy sighed as she watched a convertible full of what looked like college girls cruising the strip down below, calling out to a group of guys on the sidewalk.

If people were supposed to be happy alone, then why were they always looking to hook up? Of course, that was the part that no one was supposed to talk about—that being alone was perfectly fine in theory, but in practice, it left something to be desired.

Namely, companionship. Sex. Affection.

Macy had to believe those things weren't too much to want. But they were too much to want with the wrong guy.

Determined not to let her thoughts get any more morose, she left the balcony and went inside, got into her nightgown and crawled into bed with the latest Nora Roberts book, which she'd been saving for just this type of occasion. If she couldn't have true love of her own right now, at least she could experience it vicariously.

When she heard a knock at her door, Macy blinked at the ceiling, disoriented. She must have dozed off, she thought. But then it registered that it was actually daylight in the room, not nighttime. Which meant she must have slept all night. Her book was beside her on the bed, and the bedside lamp was still on. She must have been exhausted for the light not to have woken her up in the middle of the night.

Must have been housekeeping knocking on the door.

Macy glanced at the clock and saw that it was almost eight o'clock. A little early for housekeep—

Almost eight o'clock, and she had a meeting with the Golden Gate execs at eight-thirty. She bolted upright in bed, her heart racing. She still had to shower, get ready, review the presentation materials....

And then there was the person at the door to deal with, too. Macy got out of bed and called, "Just a minute."

She crossed the room to the door and peered out the peephole, expecting to see a woman with a cleaning cart. Instead she saw Griffin.

Griffin?

Macy's belly flip-flopped, and her breath caught in her throat. This was the last thing she needed to deal with right now. Griffin, here to remind her what a horrible person she was? Here to tell her he'd changed his mind and wasn't leaving after all? Here to reclaim his rightful place running the account? Griffin, here to...what? What could he possibly have been in Las Vegas for?

"Macy? Could you open the door? I can see your shadow through the peephole. I need to talk to you."

She put her hand on the doorknob but couldn't seem to make herself turn it. "So talk. I'm listening."

"I need to see your face to say what I have to say."

Macy looked down at her nightgown. He'd seen her in a lot less. She took a deep breath and let it out. She was terrified of facing the one person she'd failed the most, the person who'd seen her at her ugliest.

Facing him again would mean facing her failure, but

more important, it would mean facing the temptation to settle for less than her ideal guy again. That is, if he was still even interested in her.

"Macy?"

She pulled the door open. "What are you doing here?"

He smiled. "I talked to Carson last night. He told me you were giving the big presentation this morning, so I caught the red-eye out here to help you prep this morning."

She tried to think of something to say, but nothing came to mind. He'd flown out here just to help her? Not likely. Not Griffin.

"What's your ulterior motive?"

He grinned, busted. "Can I come in before I tell you?"

"No."

"Please?"

Macy rolled her eyes and stepped aside, then closed the door behind him. His presence was at least welcome to her senses, which went on alert at his nearness. His scent nearly made her swoon, and she tried to breathe through her mouth to avoid becoming too intoxicated.

"You don't look like you're all ready to go into the big meeting. Or is this your latest business attire?"

"I overslept, smart ass. Your knock woke me up."

But that reminded her, time was ticking away. If she skipped the shower, she could probably get ready in fifteen minutes instead of an hour, so that's what she'd have to do.

"Good thing I arrived then, eh?"

"If you don't mind, I'm going to get dressed in the bathroom. You can talk to me through the door," she said as she opened the closet and pulled out her overnight bag and her suit.

"Wait," he said. "I just need five minutes of face time. If you want me to leave after that, I'm gone. Okay?"

She dropped her stuff in the bathroom and turned back to him.

"Are you trying to sabotage me now?"

"I'm not the one who launched the big sabotage campaign in this relationship."

She winced. Oh, right. That was apparently her expertise.

"I'm sorry," she said.

"I forgive you. For everything. Okay?"

Her throat tightened, forcing her to nod in response. He was making this too easy. She deserved more of his wrath.

He continued. "I don't care how we started out. All I know is that I want you, and I'm not going to be happy until I have you. If you don't feel the same way, I'll turn around right now and walk away and never see you again."

She shook her head, wishing she could erase all the damage she'd done. "I'm sorry, Griffin. I just don't see us working out in the long run."

"Why? Because I don't fit some preconceived notion of the kind of guy you're supposed to be with? Because I'm not your dark, brooding romance hero? I've got to tell you Macy, what you're holding out for is a fantasy, not a real guy."

She blinked, shaking her head, unable to produce a proper defense.

"You need to forget about all that and let me be the guy you need. Because I am. You need someone who sees how amazing you are, someone who doesn't care about your flaws because to him they're not flaws at all, someone who's as crazy about you as I am."

His words sank in, and Macy tried to think of a proper argument. But... He was making a hell of a lot of sense. Was she really looking for a guy who didn't exist?

No way.

"I've dated guys just like what you described. I know they're out there."

His eyebrow cocked. "Oh, really? So why aren't you with any of them now?"

"Because they weren't the right guy."

"Because they weren't me."

"You're just my high-school fantasy," she said, turning toward the bathroom. "You're the kind of guy I wanted before I knew better."

But he caught her hand in his, and in one fell swoop she was somehow up against him, pressed against the wall. He took both her hands in his and lifted them up over her head. And he kissed her like they might never have another chance.

Like this was the last kiss in the history of the universe.

The feel of his lips coaxing hers into submission, the feel of his tongue against hers, the friction of his skin, the heat of his body, the firmness of his touch, all worked their magic on her. And she knew, no freaking way could this be the last kiss.

This was her wakeup call.

She had to stop going around wishing for things she didn't really need and looking for the things she did. Like Griffin. She needed him. Her body needed him. Her soul needed him.

She finally understood what was missing from her life—all the stuff she was afraid of. All the stuff she couldn't control. All the risky stuff.

Griffin was one of those guys she couldn't control, and she was an idiot for not seeing that as the benefit it was. Who wanted a man willing to live under her thumb?

Who wanted a fictional guy, a romance-novel hero who brooded too much and said only the things the author made him say? He was an illusion, and Griffin was real.

And maybe that had been the problem. She'd spent too much time looking for a guy who could measure up to an impossible standard. And she'd spent too much time obsessing over her teenage angst. Lauren had, of course, been right about that.

She felt herself melting against his heat. Her body, her desire, her will to resist, all melted away. Left in their place was only this kiss, and when she broke it, she couldn't let him go on thinking she was still holding out for anything less than him.

"I'm sorry, Griffin. I want you more than I can say."

He smiled as he traced his fingers along her jawline and down her neck, sending tingles through her.

"Are you sure?"

"I should be asking you that."

"I've never been so sure of a woman in my life as I am of you. I love you, Macy. No getting around it."

"I love you, too," she said, and the words came out so easily, so full of certainty, she knew then that they'd been true for longer than she'd been willing to admit to herself.

"There's one more thing. I've decided to strike out on my own, start a new agency and see what happens."

"Wow." Macy blinked at the news. "Are you sure?"

"Turning down the promotion made me think about what it is I really want in a career, and the truth is, I've never really wanted to work for someone else. I've always wanted to have complete autonomy, and I've decided I need to try working for myself before it's too late."

"There goes my fantasy of illicit meetings in the coed bathroom."

"Maybe not. Would it be too underhanded for me to hire Bronson and Wade's best talent away from them?"

"You're going to have illicit bathroom meetings with Carson?" she asked, trying not to laugh.

"With you, smart ass. Would you be interested in working with me? I mean, I know it's a big risk for you, giving up working for a prestigious ad agency to go work for an unproven one. And we'd have to work for peanuts for a while until we have a solid client base, so I understand if you wouldn't want to do it."

Macy's throat tightened. She couldn't have concocted a better thing for him to offer if she'd dreamed it up herself. If she was really going to be the kind of risk-taker she'd always dreamed of, this was her chance. Her current job was great, but like Griffin, she ached for a new challenge. Starting from scratch in a new business certainly qualified.

"I'll think about it," she said, smiling. "But first I want to know more about the compensation package. Namely, the fringe benefits."

"There would be many, many fringe benefits," he said as he bent to kiss her neck.

"Hmm," she said, relaxing into his touch. "Maybe I could just cancel the meeting, tell them I'm sick…and we could stay here all day and night."

"Another wild night in Vegas? If it turns out half as good as our last one, how could I turn it down?"

She smiled. "What happens in Vegas stays in Vegas, right?"

"No way. What happens here goes right back to San Francisco. I'm going to need a hell of a lot longer than a night with you."

She kissed him again. A month, a year, a lifetime— whatever he wanted, he could have it.

Epilogue

Three months later...

O'SHAUNNESSY'S HUMMED with its usual Wednesday-night crowd of yuppies and bar regulars. Macy, Griffin and Carson had found a table near the back of the room, where the din was low enough that they could carry on a conversation.

Carson had his eye on their pretty Irish waitress, and Macy had to resist pointing out that she'd wanted Lauren to be there. Lauren, of course, had refused, in spite of the promise that an important announcement would be made.

"So you two haven't killed each other yet," Carson said. "I'm impressed. I don't think I could run a business with a girlfriend."

Macy and Griffin glanced at each other. They hadn't really planned out how to break the news.

"We actually work better together now than we used to."

"Yeah, sex in the workplace makes everyone get along better," Carson said.

Macy made a face. "Let's don't go there."

Because she was absolutely not interested in discussing with Carson what had happened on her desk during yesterday's lunch break.

"Business is good. We've got a solid portfolio and already a waiting list of clients. Can't ask for more than that," Griffin said.

"Hey, you took your reputation with you. It's been a challenge convincing new clients that Bronson and Wade is still a solid agency."

"You still loving life as the boss man?" Griffin asked.

Carson leaned back in his chair, looking pleased with himself. "Not that it was easy taking over a creative team whose two strongest members had just quit…"

"Yeah, yeah. We're so sorry."

Macy had been conflicted about whether or not to jump into a new business venture with Griffin, but in the end she just kept coming back to the fact that she wanted the challenge. That's why she'd wanted the creative director job so badly, and with that door closed to her, she just couldn't turn down the chance to do something exciting and new. Especially when it was with the man she loved.

She'd been terrified that they'd fall back into their old adversarial habits, but Carson was right, sex had a way of diffusing even the most frustrating disagreements.

And now that she knew Griffin better, it wasn't hard to see past his seemingly arrogant facade.

"You think your friend Lauren's ever going to return my calls?" Carson asked.

Macy shrugged. "I don't pretend to understand her. She's extremely opposed to commitment."

"I don't need a commitment. I just want to see her again."

"Sorry. If I were you, I'd give up and pursue other options."

The waitress arrived then and placed their drinks on the table.

"Case in point," Macy said.

Carson eyed the woman appreciatively, but made no move to get her attention. When the waitress disappeared again, Griffin shook his head.

"You're a shell of your former self, dude," he said.

"I know. It's pretty damn sad, really. I just can't stop thinking about Lauren. She's completely different from any other woman I've been with."

Macy felt awful for having been the cause of their meeting in the first place, but she'd learned better than to play matchmaker.

"Forget me, though," Carson said. "You said you had some important announcement to make."

Griffin cleared his throat as he sat up a little straighter. He glanced at Macy again, his gaze full of some secret happiness. He'd been looking like that for days, and it took her breath away. She loved seeing a guy like him, usually so cocky and sure of himself, brought a little more down to earth by something as simple and complicated as love.

"I proposed to Macy yesterday," he said. "And she accepted."

Carson smiled. "Awesome! That calls for a toast," he said, holding up his beer.

Griffin and Macy followed suit.

"To the best couple I know—a long, happy life together," Carson said, and they clinked their bottles together, then drank.

Macy felt the sting of tears in her eyes. She blinked

them away. She'd been getting unexpectedly emotional at odd moments ever since the incident on her desk yesterday, when after a round of particularly passionate lovemaking that had scattered three days' worth of filing on the floor and broken a cute pink coffee mug, Griffin had uttered those most unexpected words.

Let's get married.

She hadn't even hesitated. She'd just said yes. She'd blinked away tears, and she'd known without a doubt that she wanted Griffin to be her husband more than she'd ever wanted anything. She was finally going to have her own happily ever after.

"So do I get to be in the wedding?" Carson asked.

"I believe there's a best man position that needs to be filled," Griffin said.

"I'm there, man. You planning a quick wedding?"

"We haven't picked a date. We're trying to figure out where we want to go on a honeymoon, and when we can swing it with our current client load and then we'll go from there."

Macy's gaze met Griffin's, and they smiled at each other. She was filled with the kind of bone-deep satisfaction that came with finding one's destiny and following it, risks be damned.

* * * * *

Look for the next book by
Jamie Sobrato!
Coming in October 2006
from Harlequin Blaze

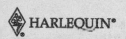

**Hidden in the secrets of antiquity,
lies the unimagined truth...**

Introducing

a brand-new line filled with mystery
and suspense, action and adventure,
and a fascinating look into history.

And it all begins with DESTINY.

In a sealed crypt in
France, where the
terrifying legend of
the beast of Gevaudan
begins to unravel,
Annja Creed discovers
a stunning artifact
that will seal her destiny.

*Available every other
month starting
July 2006, wherever
you buy books.*

GRA1

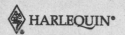

HARLEQUIN®

American ROMANCE®

American Beauties

SORORITY SISTERS, FRIENDS FOR LIFE

Michele Dunaway

THE MARRIAGE CAMPAIGN

Campaign fund-raiser Lisa Meyer has worked
hard to be her own boss and will let nothing—
especially romance—interfere with her success.
To Mark Smith, Lisa is the perfect candidate for
him to spend his life with. But if she lets herself
fall for Mark, will she lose all she's worked for?
Or will she have a future that's more than
she's ever dreamed of?

On sale August 2006

Also watch for:

THE WEDDING SECRET
On sale December 2006

NINE MONTHS NOTICE
On sale April 2007

Available wherever Harlequin books are sold.

Stability is highly overrated....

Dana Logan's world had always revolved around her children. Now they're all grown up and don't seem to need anything she's able to give them. Struggling to find her new identity, Dana realizes that it's about time for her to get "off her rocker" and begin a new life!

Off Her Rocker

by Jennifer Archer